UNNATURAL HABITATS
& OTHER STORIES

Unnatural Habitats

& OTHER STORIES

Angela Mitchell

**wtaw
press**

Publications by WTAW Press—a not-for-profit literary press—are made possible by
the assistance received from individual donors.

Designed by adam b. bohannon
Edited by Peg Alford Pursell
Author photo by Jacoby Andrick

PUBLISHER'S CATALOGING-IN-PUBLICATION DATA
Names: Mitchell, Angela M., author.
Title: Unnatural habitats and other stories / Angela Mitchell.
Description: Santa Rosa, CA: WTAW Press, 2018.
Identifiers: ISBN 978-0-9988014-6-9 | LCCN 2018933253
Subjects: LCSH Ozark Mountains Region--Fiction. | Rural conditions--Fiction. |
Crime--Fiction. | Criminals--Fiction. | Mountain life--Fiction. | Missouri--Fiction. |
Arkansas--Fiction. | Short stories, American--Ozark Mountains Region. | Southern
States--Social life and customs--Fiction. | United States--Social life and customs--
Fiction. | BISAC FICTION / General
Classification: PS3613.I85 U66 2018 | DDC 813.6--dc23

Manufactured in the United States of America and printed on acid-free paper.

To Robert, for taking the hard way with me
& In memory of Marilyn, who told the best stories

CONTENTS

ANIMAL LOVERS

It was stupid to ask for the dogs. Dee had done it on impulse, when the excitement of getting divorced was starting to wear off. "I want full custody," she told Carter. "The same as if we had kids."

"I guess I don't care," he said. Carter was cleaning out the front closet, and he sat back on his heels. "If you think you can handle it, then you can take them. It'll just make life easier on me." The dogs, Ralph and Mickey, lay together in their crate, curled up in an endless circle of fur. Mickey raised his head at the sound of Carter's voice, then gave a snort and went back to sleep.

"Okay, good," she said. "I just wanted to get that straight." It might have been nice if Carter could've acted a little more upset, but Dee let it go. She'd been the one to ask for the divorce, bringing it up one night when they'd gone out for Mexican. It was January then and the first snow of the year had fallen over the hills of Fayetteville, silencing the town until the warm earth beneath began to melt the ice and cold away. Dee had lived in Arkansas all her life, where everyone stayed inside until the snow was nearly gone.

"What the hell, Dee? Where did this come from?" Carter asked, when she told him she'd already seen an attorney.

She licked the salt from the rim of her glass, and her face

puckered as she told him the truth. "I never wanted to get married in the first place. I was all mixed up even before the wedding."

"But you cried during our vows."

"I know, but I was caught up in the moment," she said, digging a tube of lip balm out of her purse. She loved the margaritas at Jose's, but the salt made her lips burn. "You know, the dresses and the flowers and that Bible passage they read and all? It was like crying at a movie."

"The dresses?" Carter looked at her like she was crazy, but by then the waiter had returned and was standing over them, refilling the salsa bowl. Dee smiled at the waiter. "Brown Eyed Girl" played in the background, a song she enjoyed imagining was just for her. When she turned back around, Carter had his face in his hands and she dropped her head down to see if he was crying. He wasn't, but that was all right. It might've been embarrassing to have him cry right there at Jose's. Carter sat up and rubbed his nose, then picked up a tortilla chip and put it in his mouth. "What the hell, Dee?" he said again, mumbling as he chewed.

But now Carter was fine with the divorce and had even been cooperative about the division of goods. They'd talked it over and decided the best thing was to pile up all the junk they didn't want and have a garage sale. They'd split the money and whatever hadn't sold. "As long as we're calling dibs, though, I'd like to have the crystal," he said. "And the china. I love that china."

What kind of man loves china? Dee thought, but agreed to let him have it. It was ugly anyway. She'd picked it out her-

self, thinking its geometric pattern was styl.
knew better. In ten years, no one would wa
the type of china you kept for a lifetime; it
you'd pass down to your children.

Not that Dee had wanted to have children   ...ter.
And maybe this was why, because she knew she'd never
want to get pregnant by a man like him, one who honestly
valued china or silverware or the crystal goblets for which
she'd so foolishly registered. She and her mother had floated
around Dillard's creating her registry, greedily checking off
each item she thought she needed, chattering at the sales
girl who'd been assigned to help them. It became a weekly
ritual after that, the two of them roaming the department
store, snooping through the gift registry to see what was left
to receive. It was like winning the lottery over and over.

All this when Dee was still going out with Shelly at night,
hanging out at some dark table, drinking and making eye
contact with losers. She and Shelly had lived together for
six years, ever since they both quit Tri-Delt sophomore year
and moved off campus. Dee was dating Aaron then, her boy-
friend from high school, whom she'd assumed she would
marry. Between Aaron and Carter, Dee had slept with a lot
of men, though she hadn't intended to do so. She'd intended
to remain a virgin until her wedding day, a goal that seemed
impractical by the time she started dating Aaron. He'd made
it clear she didn't have many options when it came to sex:
she could do it and he'd be quiet, or she could not do it
and he'd tell everyone she had. Sex was a funny thing, she
learned. There was no going back once you started.

It was easy for her to get men to pay attention to her, which was strange, because Shelly was prettier, what with her golden brown hair, her good skin, her blue eyes. In comparison, Dee had the appearance of a woman who was merely trying to look sexy, but it worked. Even the night before her wedding, she'd flirted, successfully, with several men at the bar, later meeting one at his apartment when everyone thought she was home getting her rest for the big day. Men never talked to Shelly if Dee was around.

"It's about the vibe," she'd told her friend on that final night as a single woman, the bachelorette party having fizzled out early. "You don't put out the right vibe, the one that says you're available."

"But you're not available, technically," Shelly whined. "I think it's all bullshit."

"Oh, yes, I am available," she said. "Right up until I get that ring on my finger."

"You have a ring on your finger already." Shelly pointed to the diamond Carter had given Dee. He'd opted for size over quality, knowing she would prefer something flashy.

"This isn't the one that counts," she said, wiggling the fingers of her left hand. "This one's just a gift."

Once Carter was done with the closets, the two of them straightened up the garage and set up tables cobbled together out of sawhorses and plywood. The real estate agent told them to get rid of as much extra furniture and clutter as they could. Most of what they put out for the sale was brand-new, some of it from the wedding two years before and never taken out of the box. Dee started to price those items a little higher, then thought better of it. The important thing was to make sure it all sold.

The day of the sale, there was a layer of frost still on the lawn when Carter opened the garage door, a dozen or more shivering bargain-hunters standing in the driveway. By noon, they'd carried off nearly everything.

No sooner than they'd put the "For Sale" sign out in the yard, it was all over, except for scrubbing down the house for the new owners, and, of course, the sex. Their sex life as a couple had been dead for months, but strangely, agreeing to divorce had invigorated their desire for one another. After they'd decided to stay in the house together until it sold, they'd started having sex almost every night, then showering separately and returning to the bed to read or watch TV until they fell asleep.

The dogs slept in their crate in the kitchen, though that hadn't been the plan when they first got them. Dee wanted the dogs to sleep with her and Carter, wanted them to stretch their warm, yellow bodies along her legs and over her feet, but Ralph and Mickey couldn't be trusted. The first night she tried it, the dogs stayed at first, snuggling in, but later she woke to the sound of something like a giant zipper being pulled and found the dogs in the living room, tearing up the drapes.

"Why do we do this?" she asked Carter the night before they both moved out. She stood at the door of the bathroom, a towel wrapped around her body, and pulled a wide-toothed comb through her wet knot of tangles. She'd over-highlighted her hair and even when she used conditioner, the strands felt like the dense clumps that had to be cut from the dogs' manes.

"What?" Carter looked up from the *Cosmo* he was reading. Dee had a stack of them set aside to go to recycling, but he'd found them and taken them for his own.

"I don't know why we have sex like we do. We don't even like each other."

"I still like you."

"You shouldn't, though," she said. "It's not normal. And this sex isn't normal, either."

Carter put the magazine down and tipped his head back to look at the ceiling, pausing to think. "Maybe it's sort of like storing up for the winter," he finally said. "Maybe it's like we know we probably won't be getting it much for a while, so we're just getting what we can now before it's too late."

"Like squirrels?" she said.

"Like sex squirrels," he said and laughed.

"Forget I asked." She grabbed a bottle of moisturizer. Her skin was dry, too, probably from going to the tanning bed. She rubbed a palmful of lotion over her arm and looked back at Carter, the sheet pulled primly over his body, tucked in close to his sides. Her attorney said the papers would be ready to sign by the end of the month, finalizing the divorce. But it seemed unnecessary, really, the legality of their parting. She'd hardly felt married at all these past two years and, oddly, she'd realized it was the fantasy of being divorced, the dream of leaving that made being with Carter as long as she had even possible. Sometimes, she watched Ralph and Mickey with a kind of envy. She and Carter had bought two crates for them, but the dogs refused to be separated. They slept together in a lovers' embrace, one's head nestled into the neck of the other, their front legs folded in at their bellies, their back ones intertwined.

In all the nights she'd slept with Carter, she'd never once longed for him that way. In fact, when his hand or leg brushed against hers, her sleeping body, rather than move closer, instinctively recoiled.

Now here she was, free of Carter and the house and the junk, the cold days of the long spring gone at last, and it was the dogs who were ruining her life. Dee hadn't bothered to even look for a new place until they had a contract on the house, not realizing how few choices were available. If it weren't for the dogs, she could've moved into one of the brand-new apartment buildings in Fayetteville or Springdale, where there were probably loads of other single people living, a place where she could meet somebody and fall in love. Instead, she'd backed herself into a corner with the dogs, making it so that she had to rent a house with a fenced lot. A nicer house would've been too expensive. The houses on Garland Avenue were all at least fifty years old and this alone kept the rents low. On either side of the ugly chain-link that encompassed Dee's backyard, there were college students living in the other run-down houses, and she felt ridiculous watching them come and go, the lineup of cars in their driveways changing by the hour.

From the looks of the trim work around the doors and the bottoms of the cabinets, Dee knew Ralph and Mickey weren't the first animals to live in the house, but in practically no time, they'd managed to create fresh damage of their own. The move had upset their routine, throwing them back into their worst habits. Ralph's stomach was having problems—no telling what he'd eaten—and she took him outside to poke an Imodium down his throat. The whole house was carpeted, so he'd have to stay out until the diarrhea passed. When she came back in, she heard the sound of cracking and found Mickey in the bathroom, tearing a cabinet door off with his teeth.

"Stop that." She pulled Mickey away from the door. He growled at her as she stuck her fingers between his jaws, yanking out a chunk of wood. When the time came to move, the landlord would nail her for this one. "What the fuck," she said, tossing the wood chunk in the trash. Next door, a row of cars had collected in front and she could hear the kids screaming at each other, setting up for a party. The dogs' crate took up too much room in the small house, but since it had turned warm, she kept it in the backyard, which was fine unless it was a party night. On a party night, Ralph would howl until one of the kids came over with a bowl full of beer, straight from the keg. They'd open the door of the crate and Ralph would lap up the beer and fall asleep, then eat a load of grass the next morning and throw up.

She sat down on the toilet lid and put her face in her hands. She'd have never gotten the dogs in the first place if Carter hadn't started in talking about babies. Panicked, she'd said, "Let's go to the pound. I've always wanted a dog and it would be good practice for parenthood, right?"

"I guess it could be," Carter said, unconvinced.

They went to PetSmart on adoption day and stood in front of the cages. Carter poked his fingers through the door of one, stroking the nose of a rusty-colored coonhound. "I like this one," he said dreamily, though Dee wrinkled up her nose. It looked too much like her father's old hunting dog. When he was angry, her father kicked that dog, one time pummeling it all the way down the front steps of the house, even as it lost control of its bowels.

Then Dee saw Ralph and Mickey, both dogs half-golden retriever, half-unknown, a mystery represented by two giant question marks on their information card. "Prefer to be adopted together," the card said, and Dee liked this, the idea that they belonged to each other. The dogs frantically pushed their black noses through the wire of their pen, whimpering as they danced back and forth. Their owner had given them up when he moved, claiming they were wonderful pets, but he would be living in an apartment and it wouldn't be fair to make them live that way without a yard to enjoy.

"I think he was getting a divorce and just didn't want to tell us," the adoption woman whispered as she took Dee and Carter's application. "We get that a lot, people breaking up and giving their animals away." What they discovered when they got home was that the dogs had behavioral issues. They yowled into the night and had accidents on the floor, even when they'd been out for walks three or four times a day. The dogs chewed through anything—a corner of linoleum popped up from the floor, the closet doors, the leg of the coffee table. They were sick nearly all the time. Mickey had once vomited for two days straight until whatever had made him ill exhausted itself, and the dog lay thin and dehydrated in the living room, his feet tucked under the couch.

It wasn't just avoiding the subject of a baby, though, that caused Dee to want the dogs. She was bored, too. Bored with Carter and the house and her job, and it didn't matter what she bought or how many different ways she rearranged the furniture or what she did with her hair, she couldn't stop being bored. Sometimes in the evening, she'd walk through the house, pacing in a circle, looking for something more to do, stopping in the hall or the kitchen to rest her hands on her hips and think. She'd find herself filled with an energy that was completely unfamiliar to her, a sense that she could take off down the street and run for miles. Instead, she'd sit on the couch, curling her cold feet up underneath her and staring at the wall.

Then she'd gotten fired. For five years she'd worked as the assistant to the public communications officer for the local school district. She really did do her work, but there were times when she didn't feel like typing and filing and filling in the deadlines on the giant calendar that hung on the wall. She called her mother or friends who worked at other dull jobs and talked while she rubbed layers of petroleum jelly on her hands. It hadn't mattered as long as the work eventually got done, she'd thought. But it did matter. She didn't think you could even be let go from a state job, but she walked back to her office and cleared out her desk, too shocked to protest.

Carter wasn't as sympathetic as she thought he would be. "You shouldn't have been messing around like that," he said. "But we can live off my income for a while. Take a little while and you'll find something else."

Weeks went by and she found that she enjoyed the freedom of unemployment. The dogs loved having her home, satisfied to sleep on the couch when she watched *General Hospital* or *Dr. Phil*. They didn't have to stay in their crate since she was there to let them out into the backyard, where sometimes she sat on a green resin lawn chair, warm under an afghan, watching them sniff and dig in the late fall sun, a shower of brown leaves swirling over them.

"You know, maybe you shouldn't even go back to work," Carter said to her one night. "I think this is fate's way of saying we should go ahead and have a baby. You could be pregnant by New Year's."

"I guess that's an idea," she said. Carter hadn't mentioned babies since they got the dogs and, somehow, she'd forgotten that Ralph and Mickey were only substitutes for what he really wanted. She reached her hand to her throat and felt the throb of blood pushing through her veins, a fever rising in her skin. Her stomach tensed as Ralph came up to her and dug his nose into the crotch of her jeans.

The next morning, she bought a newspaper and spread it out on the kitchen table. She found a help wanted ad for an insurance office and then took her résumé there, handing it to the man who introduced himself as Gary. Fifteen minutes later, she was hired. When she told Carter what she'd done, he was disappointed. He spent the evening slouched into the cushions of the couch, yawning and biting his thumbnail. The house felt too small and she went into the backyard with the dogs. Normally, she hated the cold, but it felt good that night, the wind burning on her cheeks, rushing up the back of her neck. The dogs walked in slow circles, taking turns licking at each other's faces and nudging their cool noses into the palm of her hand. Finally, she took them inside and put them in their crate in the kitchen.

"Did you just come in?" Carter asked, watching as she peeled off her jacket.

"God, Carter, I've been out in the yard for an hour."

"I was about to lock up," he said, stretching. "I didn't realize you were gone." Dee looked at him. They'd met through friends, not at a bar, and Shelly had been envious, since meeting a man through friends would surely bode well for a relationship. Things had fallen together and Dee had followed along and, yet, she hadn't, and she felt a darkening in her chest, a longing and a regret that could have been for Carter, but wasn't. It would be weeks before she told him she was ending the marriage, half the paperwork already done. But it was on this night, the early December wind whispering outside, the dogs asleep in their crate, she felt she had been released from Carter, as if she had both broken free and given in at the same time. The impulse to run left her then, knowing as she did that all that was left was opening the door and walking away.

In the office, Dee slumped in her chair, rubbing her fingers into the corners of her eyes. The night hadn't been restful.

Ralph's diarrhea had cleared up with the Imodium, but both he and Mickey stayed up into the early hours trading soulful howls with the partygoers next door. Before she'd left the house that morning, the dogs were dead asleep and didn't even notice when she opened the crate door and refilled their food and water.

She took a sip of her Diet Coke and flipped on her computer. Her job consisted mostly of typing up proof-of-insurance cards and taking payments at In-Sure U. It was high-risk auto insurance. "They're paying out the nose for this coverage," Gary explained when he hired her. "They've all been dumped by State Farm and American Family, so now they're down to us." Gary wasn't the boss, though. That was Layton, a man Gary's age who almost never came out of the back room. It was only the three of them in the office— Layton to do the books, Dee to answer phones and process paperwork, and Gary to do whatever it was he did. Work was better when Gary was around. Without Carter, her life had grown quieter than she expected, but Gary broke up the silence, making jokes about people who walked by the office front on their way to the martial arts studio next door. The two of them spent the afternoons listening to shouts and grunts and barefooted smacks against vinyl, Gary doing mock karate chops in the air. When he was gone, Dee was so lonesome and bored, she was tempted to put her head down and sleep.

Gary plopped himself down on the edge of her desk, snapping his fingers in front of her face. She liked having him so close, close enough she could smell him. He was handsome in his own way, his pale brown hair shaggy around his ears, the stubble on his jaw coming in red. He must have had horrible acne when he was young by the looks of the scars on his cheeks, but they'd faded enough that now they gave him a certain masculine character. He didn't wear a T-shirt under his polo and she could see the outline of his torso. He was thinner than Carter. Thin like a runner, she thought. She could get used to a runner. He waved a finger at her head. "You use a lot of hairspray, don't you?"

She reached up to her hair. "I don't think so." She sneered at him and turned to her computer, angry he'd messed up her sexy thoughts about him. It seemed that Carter had been right about the gloomy future of singlehood, and sexy thoughts were all she had.

"I'm not saying it's bad," he said. "I'm just saying it looks kind of crunchy, you know. It's a little unnatural."

"I don't give a shit about what's natural." Shelly criticized her hair, too, saying the cut wasn't very professional, but what was? Dee liked to pull the shorter layers up on top of her head and knot them off with a rubber band, creating a fountain of hair. It seemed to lift up her face, slimming it and making her eyes look wider, more exotic.

She shooed him off her desk, then she brought up her e-mail. Now that she didn't have Carter's income to fall back on, she couldn't take as many risks on the job and avoided personal calls. It was less conspicuous to e-mail, though she noticed it took up just as much time as talking on the phone and she was having to stay a little later at the office to get through her filing. It was only Dee and Layton then. Some-

times a man would come in, asking to see Layton and looking nervously past her. She didn't like to knock on Layton's
door herself, so she'd send the man on back, where he'd announce himself in a whisper and slip inside. Gary had told
her not to bother Layton if she could keep from it, to always
step lightly. "He's got a lot going on," he said. "Don't want
him biting your head off."

But she'd figured out this was also the time when Layton
sat in his office and smoked weed. Sometimes she heard
other voices and the sound of car doors opening and clos-
ing in the back alley. Throughout the day, she was certain
she could smell marijuana, the sweet, burnt scent lingering
in the carpeting or a whiff of it caught on a piece of paper
that Layton had signed. At night, she swore she'd brought
the smell home with her, pulling her shirt off and holding it
close to her nose, inhaling as deeply as she could. It seemed
strange, someone being so careless, and it worried her a little. Still, it wasn't like he was asking her to run deliveries,
driving vacuum-sealed bags of drugs over into Oklahoma or
down to Little Rock. Maybe that was what Gary did? That
would explain the days he was gone, times when he said he
was out investigating claims.

"He's not checking out claims," Shelly said. Dee had wanted to ask Gary to go to lunch with her, but after he started in
on her hair, she asked Shelly instead. "They don't even do it
like that anymore, send out adjusters to talk to people. They
just take pictures and shit."

"And how would you know so much?"

"I just had that wreck last year," Shelly answered, picking

at her salad. "I've totaled two cars in five years and I've never met an adjuster yet."

"Well, people make claims; I see the paperwork. It's just a small business, so maybe Gary and Layton believe in good customer service, doing things the old way," she said.

"And maybe you're just blind because Gary's hot. I think it's throwing off your instincts." Shelly looked at her and smiled.

Dee looked down at her hands. She'd gotten rid of Carter's diamond after the divorce, trading it in for a thick, silver band set with an aquamarine, her birthstone. The first day she took off her wedding rings, her hand felt weightless, as if it could float away. It was like the old trick she did as a girl, standing in a doorway, pushing her hands against the frame as hard as she could, then stepping away and watching as her arms lifted up, up, out of her control.

She squinted her eyes at Shelly and reached over to pick a tomato off her plate. "Whatever," she said. "I don't think I even have instincts."

Ralph and Mickey needed exercise—that was the problem—but Dee wasn't very interested herself. She'd taken one of the two TVs she and Carter had owned when she moved to the house on Garland and set it up on a dresser in her bedroom. It was a pleasure to crawl into bed after work and flip through the channels with no one to interrupt her. She'd always passed over the PBS station before, but a program on dogs caught her attention. The show was part of a fundraising marathon. She hated when they stopped to ask for money, but she loved the special. On one episode, the host explained that dogs were like children, prone to cause trouble if they couldn't release their extra energy. It wouldn't hurt her to get more exercise, either, she admitted. For the first time in her life, the backs of her thighs were beginning to ripple with cellulite.

She bought stronger leashes and two choke collars. She imagined herself walking down the street, Ralph and Mickey clipping along beside her, happy at last, no longer stupidly cocking their heads to the side when she gave a command. *You are the alpha dog, the leader of the pack,* the man on the PBS special had said. *You must demonstrate a calm, assertive nature.* Ralph and Mickey nipped at her when she put the chokes over their noses and ears, then they tried to jerk away from her as she snapped on their leashes.

"Now," she said, standing tall and straight the way the dog trainer had said to do. "Let's go for a walk." Ralph and Mickey looked confused as she pulled them out the door and they pushed their bodies closer together, sinking their weight into their legs. They refused to walk, so she stepped out in front of them, yanking at the chokes. Without any real direction from her, they seemed to understand.

They walked past the first three houses, the dogs trotting at an ideal pace. She nodded confidently at a jogger across the street. At the end of the block, a group of young men gathered in front of a house with a broad porch, half the rail spindles busted out. One of them looked back at her and, motioning to his friends, pointed toward her with his beer can. She smiled at the men, pleased that she'd won control of the dogs, shocked though she was at how easy it had come. *It's all about the vibe,* she whispered, lifting her chin a little higher.

She saw the chipmunk first, standing at the base of the maple in the next yard. Ralph and Mickey loved chipmunks and she'd seen them jointly go on the attack for one in the backyard, running so hard in pursuit they hit the fence, knocking themselves dizzy. The trainer hadn't said anything about chipmunks. Maybe he didn't mention it because it shouldn't matter. Once control was asserted by the master, did the dog surrender his own desires? Maybe there was no such thing as only partial submission. The dogs slowed and sniffed the air. She began to pray a silent prayer in her head: *Oh, Heavenly Father, please don't let these stupid dogs see that goddamn chipmunk. Please, don't let it move.*

The chipmunk made a break for the bushes beside the house, a black and brown zip across the yard. Ralph and Mickey stood still, each raising a paw, their bodies posed in a pointer's stance. Then they leaped, together, into the grass, yanking her along with them. "Stop," she said. "Hold!" The rough braid of the leashes burned down over her wrists and hands. She ran along with the dogs, trying to make the sound in her throat that the man on the PBS special made, the screeching, throaty grunt that was supposed to get their attention, but Ralph and Mickey weren't listening. They lunged forward in an attempt to break away, the two of them using all their strength, and she fell, still holding the leashes. The dogs barely slowed at all. At last, she let go, the leashes slapping like whips behind Ralph and Mickey as they ran.

The chipmunk had vanished and, without her to hold them back, the dogs redirected themselves, gleefully aware of their freedom and forgetting the hunt entirely. Traffic was heavy on Garland and, as she lay in the grass and dirt, she hoped the dogs might get hit. She ran her tongue over her teeth, tasted the salt of her own blood. The dogs turned the corner at North Street—amazingly, they stayed on the sidewalk—and she did not call after them.

She limped back to the house. Maybe the dogs would get picked up by someone, then dumped at a shelter or out in a farmer's field. She'd certainly considered doing this herself, but she didn't have the nerve. The dogs' collars with their tags lay on the kitchen table; she'd taken them off before she'd slipped on the chokes. No one could trace the dogs back to her and she was relieved, though she wished she could get her money back for the choke collars. She'd bought the best she could find, nearly fifteen dollars apiece. Thirty dollars was a lot of money for something that ran away.

When she awoke the next morning, she started for the back door to let the dogs in and remembered they were gone. She smiled and headed to the refrigerator for a Diet Coke. The cold can numbed the palms of her hands, soothing the bruises, and she sighed as she sipped her drink. She had a couple of hours before she had to be at the office, so she went back to bed and turned on the TV, stretched out and closed her eyes. Then she heard something—a whining sound, punctuated by scratching and popping thumps against the siding. She got up and looked through the shades. They were back, Ralph and Mickey in the yard, digging together at the base of the fence, which they had already squeezed under to come home. Clods of dirt and grass flew all around them. Dee turned away from the window, leaned her back against the wall, and slid down to the floor. She felt as close to crying as she had in years.

"You're looking good this morning," Gary teased her at the office. Dee's elbows and hands had gotten scraped in the fall, but so had her nose, and she looked as if she had food on it, like she'd been eating chocolate pudding with just her face. Attempting to cover it with makeup and powder had only made the scabs more apparent.

"I'm getting rid of my fucking dogs," she said, sitting down at her desk. Typing was going to be murder. The muscles of her hands ached from holding the leashes so tight.

"You never said you had dogs," Gary said. "You don't seem like a dog person."

"I'm not." She could swear she smelled dog shit and she pulled her shoes off to check them. They were clean, but she couldn't escape the smell. "That's why they're going."

"Well, don't take them to a shelter," he said. "That's a death sentence for an animal."

"Listen, I need to get to work." She cut her eyes at him. "So unless you want the dogs, don't bother me. I've done all I can do."

Dee ate lunch at her desk and Googled "animal shelters," making a list to call. There was only one inside the Fayetteville city limits, another out near Elkins. The rest were dedicated to cats alone. She considered Gary's words, how he'd said to let him know before she got rid of the dogs. He'd been away much of the morning and, lonely for his company, she decided to forgive him for making her feel guilty about Ralph and Mickey. She was finishing the last bite of her sandwich when she heard the door in back open and close.

"I'm back now," he said. Gary settled himself at his desk against the wall and pulled out his cell phone. "I don't guess anyone's been in, have they? A guy?"

"No, not today," she said. "I need to talk to you."

"About what?" he asked, not looking up from his phone. "Just a second."

He pressed a finger to his brow, then put the phone in his pocket. He let out a deep breath and rolled his chair across the room to sit beside her. "What is it?"

"My dogs," she said. "I've got to do something." Not only were the dogs driving her crazy, she explained, keeping her in a run-down house she hated, they were getting expensive, too. How come she hadn't noticed how much dog food cost before? And giving them back to Carter was out of the question. His apartment didn't allow pets of any sort. "You said to talk to you before I took them to a shelter."

"Well." He smoothed his hair back off his forehead and stretched his legs in front of him. "I've got a lot of animals already, but maybe I could take them until we find another place."

He clapped his hands as if he'd just made a discovery. "Let's do this. I'll come get you Saturday evening and drive you out to my place, in Gravette. We'll take the dogs with us, see if it works."

Unsure what to wear on Saturday night, she put on her black leggings and silver-satin tunic. Gary hadn't said it was a date, but she preferred to be overdressed than under. For going out, she always wore a little more makeup, lining her eyes with a thick, black eye pencil, making herself look like Cleopatra. Shelly thought the way she did her makeup was out of style. Natural was the fashion now, but she'd tried and it didn't look right. What was the point, anyway, of wearing makeup so it looked like you weren't? At night when she washed her face, she often thought she was nearly unrecognizable without the powder, the mascara, the lip gloss. She could almost pass for another person.

Gary got to her house early and backed his truck into the drive. He'd spread straw out on the bed and was busy arranging blankets on top of that when she walked out to tell him she was ready. "I was thinking they might do a little better if they were comfortable," he said. "Maybe they'll just go to sleep."

"I wouldn't have gone to the trouble, but thanks," she said.

His eyes drifted down her body, while he straightened the blankets. "Get the dogs and we'll go," he said.

The dogs weren't used to going anywhere and Gary had to lift them into the truck, their bodies gone stiff in his arms. Usually they barked at a stranger, but they only whimpered at him, raising their noses to lick his face. Dee pulled herself into the cab of the truck. A shotgun ran the length of the rack behind her head and she leaned her body forward so she wouldn't be close to it.

"It's not loaded," Gary said. "It's safe."

"I think it might be safer not to have it at all, but that's just me." She moved closer to the door. If it opened, she'd go flying, skidding across the highway into a ditch. She could've sat in the middle, but she still wasn't sure what Gary wanted. She let go of the door handle and tried to relax her hands in her lap.

Gravette was close to the Missouri border and it took longer to get there than she'd thought it would. She looked back at the dogs, who had settled down and huddled together in the corner of the truck bed. Once they were in Gravette, Gary weaved off the main highway, heading deep into the countryside, where the narrow road was shadowed over by the branches of trees, their leaves newly full and dark green.

Gary's house was a small split-level with gray rock along the foundation and cedar siding, so that the structure nearly blended into the yard, though he didn't have a real yard. In fact, she couldn't tell where the yard started and the surrounding woods began, the trees a thick jungle blocking out the sunlight and darkening the ground. A light wind hushed through the branches and the air was cool. To the side of the house, a clothesline held two pairs of jeans, hung by their waists.

"This is it," he said, reaching across Dee's lap to open the door, his arm brushing over her breast. "Hop on out and we'll get those dogs situated."

She dropped her feet to the gravel and stood by the truck while Gary lowered the tailgate. Ralph and Mickey stretched their backs and then stood, blinking and panting at him. He made a kissing sound and waved his arm, inviting them to jump out. Ralph, always the braver of the two dogs, wobbled at the edge of the gate before leaping to the ground. Mickey followed. The two sniffed the air.

"They'll be fine," Gary said. "I wasn't really wanting dogs, but I probably need them. They can help guard the place."

"What needs guarding?" she asked. He slipped his hand into hers and led her to the house. He rubbed his thumb on her ring.

"This is nice," he said.

"It's my birthstone." She enjoyed the touch of his fingers. How many months had it been since her last night with Carter? Only three, but it felt longer than that. It had been longer, still, since they'd kissed, their final weeks of intimacy performed without it. Kissing, they'd found, was hardly a necessity. Gary let go of her hand and unlocked the door.

"I've got my birds in the back, if you want to see them," he offered. "Two parrots and a cockatiel I got from a bird rescue."

"Birds sort of give me the creeps," she said and stepped inside the doorway. The house was plain with a few odd pieces of furniture: a couch and two chairs, a TV with a wide, flat screen. She went over by the window to an aquarium, though it didn't have water or fish, but a lizard. Another equally large aquarium stood nearby, twin snakes coiling over and through the pieces of wood and rocks inside.

"Just don't tap the glass, if you don't mind. It riles up the snakes." He moved past her toward the kitchen. "You want something to drink?"

"Whatever you've got." The temptation to tap the glass was killing her. She'd not even have thought of it if he hadn't warned her. She bent down to get a better look. One of the snakes raised its head and seemed to focus directly on her. She stepped back and felt something at her leg. Gary returned and set two bottles of beer on the table beside the couch.

"And don't be scared of Bobbie," he said. She looked down and saw the animal, a bobcat standing as high as her knees. "She's tame. I wouldn't let her be out if I thought she'd hurt you."

"Shit." She was unable make herself move. The cat pulled its face into a grimace, its wide, pink tongue visible between its teeth. When the animal moved closer, its whiskers brushed her leg. She wanted to push it away, to give it a good kick in the ribs, but she couldn't. Not with Gary watching her. Besides, a bobcat probably wouldn't be like a dog, who'd go whimpering off into the corner, terrified to ever cross you again. A bobcat would come after you, sink a nice sharp set of fangs into your leg.

"I don't think you're supposed to be keeping wild animals in your house like this."

"Bobbie's not wild. She uses a litter box."

"That's what makes her tame?"

"Sure," he said, offering his hand to the cat. It licked his fingers. "Anyway, danger's a relative thing. You've been living with the descendants of wolves. How many times have you heard of a dog flipping out and biting a kid's face off or mauling somebody to death?" He pointed out the window at the dogs. "I saw the teeth on those things," he said, looking at Dee's neck and moving closer. "One good snap there on the jugular, and that's all it would take."

Dee watched the bobcat, unsure of what to do.

"I scare the shit out of you, don't I?" Gary asked, putting his hand on her hip.

"No. Well, maybe," she said. "Are you a drug dealer? Are you selling drugs at the office?"

"We sell insurance at the office."

"But that's not all you do," she said. "My friend Shelly says you guys have something illegal going on. She worked at a restaurant once and there was all sorts of shit going on in the back room."

"Listen to me." His hand glided up to the base of her ribs. "Me and Layton have the insurance business and a thing or two on the side. It works out as long as Layton keeps it together, but sometimes he gets his own ideas." He put two fingers under her chin. "Layton fucks up, but I don't. That's why I'm there. I'm the control. Does that make sense?" He lifted her hair and sent his tongue up her neck to her ear, around to her face.

"No," she said. The bobcat flopped down on the floor beside them. Dee pulled her head to the side, away from Gary, but he caught her mouth with his thumb and drew it back to him. "Stop that," he said and kissed her.

In the night, she was certain she heard the dogs. She opened her eyes and lay still, listening. There was nothing. The moon's light slipped in through the blinds, cutting the blackness of the room with a pale ray. A body lay beside her, long and warm, and she reached over, expecting to feel Gary. Instead, she felt fur and a belly moving up and down.

"Ralph? Mickey?" But the dogs were closed up with the birds on the screened-in back porch. This body was too silky, too lean, and she pulled her hand away. Then she saw the eyes, two silver crescents in the dark. The bobcat looked over its shoulder at her and yawned, its arms draped over Gary, paws flexing. It lifted its nose in the air, grimacing again, before it relaxed its head on the mattress. Its bobbed tail beat against her leg.

Stretched out to its full length, the cat was bigger in bed. Dee wondered what it would do if she got up, if she put her clothes on and left, though she knew she wouldn't do that. Where could she go? She was somewhere she'd never been before, miles, probably, from the nearest highway, deep in the Arkansas woods. She hadn't even paid enough attention on the drive to memorize the turns of the road, the landmarks.

Gary slept on the other side of the cat, one bare leg over the top of the covers, arm tucked behind his head like a cradle. Dee hesitated, but reached her hand out and rested it on the cat's side. A sound came from its chest, neither a purr nor a growl, the echo of it vibrating across the cat's ribs. The cat thumped its tail against her one last time before settling back into sleep.

Dee was tired, too, and she sank into the pillow, her whole body giving into the quiet, and closed her eyes. She smoothed her hand along the side of the cat's chest where she could feel the throb of its animal pulse, the race of its heart faster and more familiar than she expected, something closer to her own.

NOT FROM HERE

What I did was ask if I could get off the bus to use the bathroom, but I waited until we was almost to the Clark girls' stop to do it. I didn't need to see inside the other houses, the ones that looked like my own, with a dirty kitchen and ripped up linoleum in the bathroom and a spot in the corner where the dog likes to run in and piss. I've got friends on the bus route, but most of them's got houses that aren't hardly fit to live in, truth be told, and I wanted to see a nice place for once and I knew them Clark girls wouldn't say no. And they didn't! The bus driver let me off with them and told me not to linger, but where was he going to go? He wouldn't leave me there way out in the country at some stranger's house and, besides, when we got near to the end of the bus route every day—I was the first to get on, the last to get off—he could stop the bus and I'd let him come back to my seat and kiss me and do things with his hands. The road is empty then, all the farmers gone home for supper or people who work in town not yet made it home, and he parks the bus on the side of the road so that if you was to look at it from the outside, it would seem to almost be tipping into the ditch. After you cross the creek, there's a long patch that's got trees going down to the water and more trees climbing up the other side of the ridge so the bus is kind of hid. It's quiet out there at the end of the day and I can hear the crows cawing and the blue jays fighting with the squirrels in the trees, and me and him do what we do. It could get him in a lot of trouble, but it's all right with me. He's pretty nice about it.

These girls who live in this nice house would be the kind I would like to hate, except that they don't never say anything mean to me. Instead, they get on the bus in their clean clothes with their hair fixed up right and if I put my foot out in the aisle to be ornery, they'll just say, "Excuse me, please, Libby?" I move my foot because they ask it so polite, like they don't even understand that I've just done something mean. Or maybe they don't care. Either way, I can't help but wonder what it's like to live in a house like theirs, one that's got flowers planted out front and no animals running wild, even the siding paint kept up so it's not peeling. They got a whole field full of cattle and a big barn and a chicken coop that looks about like a human being could move into it. When it's warm, they've even got this above ground pool in the backyard. All summer long, they've got it all to themselves so they don't never have to go down to the creek, risk getting bit by a cottonmouth.

When the Clark girls get sat down, I like to stare at them, especially the one who's my age and has a kind of coppery brown hair. Her name's Annette and she wears real pretty clothes, but what makes other girls jealous of her is her hair, which is long and wavy and goes most of the way down her back. One day last week, she got on the bus in the morning and sat down in the seat right in front of mine and, I don't know why I done it, but I leaned up and just breathed in, right at the back of her head. It smelled like shampoo and hairspray and a little bit of orange, which I later found out was her perfume. She got real still and then she kind of turned her head to the side like you do when you're trying hard to hear something and not get caught, but by then I'd already set back against my own seat and I pretended I hadn't just had my nose up in her hair. After that, she moved over so her shoulders was against the window and her legs stretched out over the seat, her feet dangling off the end. She had a school book out and was studying it and all I could see was the top of her head and her eyes looking down at her lap. She's like that, the type to study. The oldest sister used to ride the bus last year, but now she's off at college and I guess Annette's headed in the same direction. Maybe the younger sister, too.

But I'm not headed off to college. I don't even want to go. I like it here well enough and I've got plans to get a job soon as I get a car. There's just this year and next to get through for school and then I won't be going there everyday, where I'm bored, bored, bored, and I surely won't spend no more time on this bus. Still, it's relaxing riding the bus, and sometimes I even take a little nap, but I haven't done that since I smelled Annette Clark's hair and made up my mind I was going to start sitting behind her from now on. It's the nicest thing, this perfume she wears, too, because it don't smell like flowers or powder, like what some old lady would wear. It smells like something clean and it's made me think that I'm not sure what I smell like. Ronnie—that's the bus driver—told me that he can't smell nothing because of a job he once had at a gas station where he and the other guys pumping gas liked to take the nozzle off the hook and sniff it to feel it burn up in their heads. I told him that didn't sound very smart, but all he did was shrug and say it was a way to pass the time and, smart or dumb, I didn't smell like nothing to him. Nobody did.

At home, I shut myself in the bathroom and took off my shirt and held it up close to my nose and breathed it in, then turned it so that I could smell it at the armpit, which was stained yellow from sweat. I hadn't never noticed that before, but I hadn't noticed before that I don't smell like perfume, neither, but a little bit sour, like vinegar. My face was broke out along the chin—that's another thing about the Clarks, that they don't seem to get pimples—and I looked at myself the way maybe Annette might see me, a girl with a strange smell and yellowed armpits and a chin that looked like it'd been rubbed with gravel. You'd think it'd made me want to do something mean the way I was getting swallowed up with embarrassment and jealousy, but what boiled up in me was a terrible want to get closer to this girl. And what I needed was to see the place Annette come from, and there I'd figure out what the difference was between her and me.

I bring it up to Ronnie when he's done with me and gone back to the driver's seat. When it's just the two of us, I go sit behind him and I lean in against the safety bar and we talk. Ronnie's good at driving the bus and he said the main reason he got the job is that he don't have no convictions on his record. He said the man who does the hiring for the school said that was kind of rare, might ought to be something to be proud of. Ronnie just laughed and said, well, maybe he just ain't been caught yet, and he said the man laughed right along with him. My own dad could never be a bus driver because he *does* have a conviction on his record, over something that went on with him and my mom when I was little, some dark thing that I don't have no memory of. He says it ain't worth talking about. He's who I live with now, him and my stepmother, Gina. She's the second one I've had and I don't expect her to last, really. She says she don't like it here in Missouri and don't understand why we picked this spot of all the spots to be, way down here in the hills. It was better being poor in Oklahoma, she says, but my dad says her disability check goes farther here, so here's where we are. If it weren't for her draw, he says, we'd be up shit creek.

"Why're you so curious about that Clark girl?" Ronnie asks me, but he says it like he's suspicious, not like he's mad at me over it.

I just shrug up my shoulders and stare out the driver's window, not at Ronnie. "I'm not," I say. "I just never knew people like them."

"I can tell you this, girl. They're not your kind." We're at the bottom of a steep hill and Ronnie shifts a gear and pushes on the gas pedal real hard. When he does that, he makes this face where he pulls his lips back and shows his teeth, like he's what's making the bus engine go. I don't like it when he does that because it's ugly.

33

"What you mean?"

"I mean they're not like you and me," he says. We make it to the top of the hill and he lets his face go back to normal. There's only one more big hill to get over and then back down before we get to my house. "That family's got money. All them houses down that part of the road? It's all the same family. And all that land as far as you can see? It belongs to them, too, this big family called Dawson."

"How'd you figure that?" I say. "That Annette's part of them?"

Ronnie takes up his can of Skoal from the dashboard and rattles it at me. I open it and he tucks a dab inside his lip and rubs his tongue into it. "Let's just say I was curious myself," he says. I don't ask no more questions.

Annette don't seem to care when I ask to run in and use the toilet, so I follow her and her sister down the bus steps onto the white gravel drive. Inside the house is even better than I thought. It weren't no mansion, but Annette's family is got things like a piano and grandfather clock and this long, green velvet-looking couch with pillows that match. Above it is a real old-fashioned type mirror, where I imagine Annette checks her hair before she runs out to catch the bus in the morning and on that couch was a white cat with a black spot on its neck, just curled up in a ball like a puff of cotton. It didn't even look at me when I come in the door, it was so comfortable. My dad don't like cats, even though Gina says they'd help a lot with the mice and snakes, but he says cats have attitude problems, so he kills one as soon as it comes anywhere near. The hallway walls is covered with pictures of Annette and her sisters and even some old-time black-and-whites of people that are surely dead by now. Down at the end was another mirror, a long one, so that I can see myself head to foot, Annette behind me.

"The bathroom's right there," she says. I look at her looking at me in the mirror. She's a head taller and her face is thin compared to mine, which is round. I can't tell if she wears makeup, but I do and what's left here at the end of the day is purple eyeliner that's run so that it makes it seem like I got dark bruises under my eyes.

"All right," I say, though I don't move. Annette is real quiet standing there, and I can hear a door open somewhere in the house and then a voice call out, one I think must be her mother's. The house smells like food cooking and it hits me that I'm hungry, that I wish I could invite myself to stay.

"Are you needing something else?" says Annette. "The bus driver will start honking at you."

"I like your house. I like those pictures." I point at them and smile, not knowing what else to say. This was the most I'd ever talked to Annette and we was talking about something real, not just her asking me to move my foot. I wanted to go through the house with her and ask about every little thing I saw—the piano (did she know how to play it?), the grandfather clock (I'd never seen one up close before), the velvet couch, the white cat. I was hoping she might ask me to stay for supper, but right then I heard the bus horn honking, just like she said it would, Ronnie telling me to hurry up.

"I better go," I say.

"But you didn't even use the restroom." Annette pushes the door open and flips on the light. "I'll go tell him you just need a minute." I go on inside the bathroom and close the door and make myself at home. I touch every single thing I can.

Once I'm home, I sit down on the couch and turn on the TV. There's never anything good on this time of day, but I like to have the noise. Gina and my dad are usually home, but it seems like lately Gina's been gone a little more. She says she can't just sit here in this little house way out in the country and do nothing all day long like he can. My dad tells her that he does lots of things all day long, that he works on cars that people bring by and leave with him, salvaging out the parts that he can sell. That's how he gets his cash for cigarettes and beer and what all. Disability money's good, but it only stretches so far.

When I was in Annette's bathroom, I found a tiny bottle of perfume and I took the cap off and sprayed some on my wrists. It's the best-smelling thing I've ever come across, and while I watch TV, I keep putting my wrist up close to my nose and breathing in. There was a tray of makeup in there, too, and I thought about trying on the lipstick, but I could hear the damn bus horn laying on. I'd spent all my time playing with perfume and looking inside the drawers of the vanity, so I didn't actually get to pee, but I flushed the toilet anyway so that Annette wouldn't think I was dirty. Then I ran the water in the sink and spritzed that perfume on me one more time before I came out and fairly well ran to the bus.

My dad comes in through the back door and he lets it clang shut like he does, stomping in with his boots all clumped with mud.

"Why don't you take them things off before you come in?" I say. "You know it just makes Gina mad."

"Gina was born mad," he says. He stands there and looks at what's on the TV before he plops himself down in the chair against the wall. He makes a face and wrinkles his nose. "Are you wearing perfume?"

I shrug.

He gets up and moves over to the couch beside me. He sniffs at me again. "I asked you a question," he says. "Some boy give it to you?"

"No." I push him back. I don't like it when he gets close to me like that. "It's a girl's off the bus."

"Pretty fancy girl if she's spraying around perfume on the bus."

"It was at her house," I say, but I'm put out about having to tell my own business. What does he care if I get to wear somebody else's perfume or not? "I had to pee, so the bus driver let me off at this house where these girls live."

"I bet they didn't like having you come in to use their toilet." He's leaned away from me now and relaxed into the corner of the cushions, flat as they are. His hands are covered in oil from some engine he's supposed to be taking apart and putting back together for a friend. He could wash up, but he don't.

"It was fine. I just went in and come back out."

"And she went into the toilet with you and doused you with perfume?"

This is the last straw for me and I get up and make to go to my room. "I just tried it on myself," I say. "It was just sitting there. I'll go wash it off."

"Don't wash it off on account a me," he says. He was grinning at first, but stops and then just looks grumpy. "You want fancy things, you'll learn how to get 'em for yourself."

He's embarrassed me and I feel myself turning red in the face. "I don't want nothing."

"Well, I do," he says. He stretches out his arms up above his head and yawns, like he's been working all day. "I want some supper. Go figure out what we got. Gina don't keep up the groceries for shit."

By the next morning, Gina still hasn't come back. I go on to school like normal, but when I get off the bus that night, my dad is sitting there on the front step, looking like he could pounce.

"Gina home?" That's what he's upset about it. She comes and goes as she wants, but she's never stayed gone before.

"No."

"You called the hospitals?"

"For what?"

"She might've got herself in a accident," I say. "Remember when that happened to you?" That was in Oklahoma, when he'd slid off the asphalt in a rainstorm on a road so dark and lonely, didn't nobody find him 'til the next day. The car was done for, but he was all right, just too banged up to get his-self out.

"She didn't get in no accident. She just up and left, is what she done."

I stand there on the stoop beside him and put a hand on his shoulder, trying to be a comfort. "She might come back." What else do you say to a man whose wife is left him? With the other one, they got in a fight so loud the neighbors called it in to the police station. That wife's name was Becky and she told him to his face she was leaving. She was sick of his bullshit and she weren't never coming back. He didn't have to guess at what happened.

"I don't care if she does." He has a cigarette between his fingers, curled up under his palm so that the smoke looks to be coming out of his hand, a magic trick. "I'll miss that damn check."

"Her disability?"

"Yes, her disability," he says, mocking me. He takes the cigarette up to his mouth and sucks a long pull on it. "Not that she really got one." The smoke shoots back out his nose as he talks.

"I thought it was her heart," I say. "She said it was damaged or something."

My dad waves his hand out in front of him, brushing me away like a mosquito. "I never believed it, that heart business," he says. "I figured she just blew some crooked doctor to get that. Don't mean I didn't appreciate the money, though."

I don't like it when he talks like that around me, that sex stuff, but he mostly does it when he's low.

"You going to get a regular job now?"

"Doing what? I got that felony charge." He shoots me a real hateful look. There's times I don't like my dad, and I start counting the days until I get my car and don't have to stay here. When I have my own little house or maybe an apartment, I might even get a cat.

"Maybe you just don't tell it," I say. I was out of good advice. "We ain't from here, so who's going to know?"

Ronnie knows I'm faking it when I say I need to use the bathroom again and, here we are, just about to Annette's house. I didn't hardly sleep at all last night, what with Gina gone and my dad playing his records real loud in the front room. I'm not in the mood for nobody to give me a hard time.

"You can hold it." Ronnie stares down at me from the big rearview mirror that's tilted over his head. "You a big girl, ain't you?"

"No, I can't hold it. And I already asked Annette if I could come in again and she said it was fine."

"When'd you do that?" He knows he's not seen me talking to Annette. Ronnie sees everything that goes on. He says that's what bus drivers are supposed to do, keep an eye on everybody and make sure nobody's getting beat up or raped in the back. If he sees a fight get started, he pulls the bus off to the side of the road and then he goes back there and breaks it up, puts the kids who were fighting up in the front seat right behind him. That happened last week and the boy who got beat up so bad was bleeding out his nose. He kept wiping up the blood with his bare hand and smearing it on the wall beside him. Nobody's bothered to clean it off and the streaks of blood has turned brown.

I roll my eyes at Ronnie. I don't know why he's got to be like this. "I asked her back at school."

He lets out a little huff.

"What?" I say.

"Is she your friend now? You two sitting around at lunch together?"

"No," I say. "Maybe. She's nice."

"She's *being* nice," he says. "That don't mean she's your friend."

Annette's off in the middle of the bus with a little set of headphones on and I'm relieved that she can't hear him say none of this. I decide not to answer. Ronnie don't know everything. "I'm getting off the bus at Annette's. I drank a lot a water today and I can't hold it until I get home."

Ronnie shakes his head and stops looking at me in the mirror. He's got real dark brown eyes—so brown they're almost black—and has hair to match. The army jacket he wears is too big for him and he has to keep pushing it back off his hands, but he says it was his dad's and he don't care that it's too big and that it makes him look like a little boy in a grown man's coat. I think sometimes that he might make a good husband, but I'm not in love with him and I don't expect I will be. Still, he might be in love with me, though it's hard to tell such a thing.

We're on the dirt road now and, for meanness, Ronnie speeds up and starts hitting the big bumps. It was a hard winter and all the ice and snow has washed out big holes in the road. It's a game he plays that the kids all love and they scream for him to go faster, hit the bumps and the holes harder so that the littlest kids go bouncing out of their seats. Sometimes, they bounce so high they land back down in the aisle, which is dangerous, if you ask me. But he's doing it today to see if he can get me to pee my pants, which makes me mad enough that I get up and walk to the middle of the bus myself and sit down.

At Annette's, we stop and I look at her and mouth, "Can I?" and she nods and I follow her and her sister down the steps to the driveway. I don't even look at Ronnie, but I hear him yelling at a bunch of kids to shut up and sit down and that they are *not* going to get off the bus and go use the bathroom, too. I hadn't thought of this, that other kids would start in wanting to do the same, but what do I care? Inside Annette's house, I look for the cat, but it's not there and Annette puts her things down and points down the hallway. "You remember where it's at, right?"

I go down the hall and I'm glad that she's not following me this time because I realize that I can just poke my head in the other rooms. There's the one that's directly past the bathroom on the right and the door is open and I see that it must be her mom and dad's room because there's a woman's dress slung over the footboard. There's a little makeup table and two dressers—matching, I see—and on one is a big box that looks like it's meant to hold treasure and I think for a second about going to it and lifting the lid, but I'm afraid I'll get caught. Across the hall from this room, though, is the one I'm looking for. Its door is mostly closed and I open it just enough to see that the room is a sort of rosy pink and it smells a little like orange peels, like Annette, and I know this one is hers. There's just one bed, a small one, which means that she don't have to share with nobody. I step inside and see she's got posters on the wall of bands she likes, these men with long hair and ripped-up jeans and angry faces, and her closet door is slid open so I can see all the clothes she's got. Things are in order here and I wonder who gets this done? Is it Annette herself or her mother, who I haven't seen yet?

I can hear Annette and her sister talking in the other part of her house and it occurs to me that I haven't even made it to the bathroom yet, and so I dash on in there and close the door behind me and I'm surprised to find that now that I'm in, I really do have to go. I pull down my pants and settle onto the seat and I'm feeling so much relief, I think that I could just stay here forever in this bathroom with its wallpaper with the roses trailing down it, the shiny, green tile on the floor. I lean my head against the wall when I'm done and I close my eyes, but there's a knocking at the door and a voice real soft and polite. Nobody ever talks to me like that. "Libby," I hear Annette say, almost whispering. "The bus driver's honking again. You better hurry."

When Ronnie stops the bus in our usual place, I hold my hands up like a shield and I tell him that he might as well take me on home. He made me mad telling me that I didn't need to pee, and I'm not letting him play with me no more until he apologizes.

"What's this about?" he says, and it seems like he honestly don't know. He walks on back and stands in front of me. "You got somebody you saving yourself for?"

"You think you can tell me what to do and I don't like that."

Ronnie doesn't go back to his driver's seat, but just keeps staring at me like he's never seen anything like this, an angry girl telling him to keep his hands to hisself. He's not a very big man at all, but he's still bigger than me and, for the first time, I realize that it don't matter what I say. If he wants to do something to me, he'll do it and it won't be my choice. This has happened before—not with Ronnie, though—and I know how guys change when they done made up their mind about how things are going to go. He's got that look that says I might need to learn my place, and I cross my arms over my boobs, partly to make me seem tough and partly to hide what he's looking at. He comes closer to me and puts his hand back behind my head and I make like I'm going to bite him, but he grabs my jaw and shakes it like what I've seen my dad do to dogs. I undo my arms from my chest, trying to get his hand off my face, and he sends his other hand down my shirt and pinches me on the nipple real hard so I think I'm going to cry.

"Fine," he says. He lets go of my chin and gets his hand out of my bra. He looks around like he's afraid somebody might of snuck up and seen what he done, but there's nobody around. I press down where he pinched me, trying to make it feel better, but I bet I've got a bruise. None of this is like Ronnie, which has got me confused. "Fine," he says again. "Just tell me what it is about this Clark girl that's got you so twisted up."

I don't feel like telling him anything, but he's made it clear he's the boss. Thing is, I don't know how to answer this question because, up until a few days ago, it was really just that I was curious about Annette. I was curious about her clean hair and pretty clothes, how she got to live in one kind of way and I got to live in another. I'd seen that somebody at her house put up Christmas lights in December that came down before school started back in January and that there was a nice car sitting in the driveway and a basketball hoop with a real net over the garage door. Then I went inside and I saw that clock and the piano and the cat sleeping on the couch and, after that, I spent a lot more time than I'd like to admit thinking about what it'd be like to live there instead of with my dad and my missing stepmother. I try to tell Ronnie this, but it don't come out right because it makes it sound like I'm jealous of the stuff, which I am, but that's not why I want Annette to be my friend. Still, this is what Ronnie takes from it, that there's something I want inside that house and, if I can get my hands on it, it'll cure me of whatever's wrong.

"Wish you'd said this to start with," he says. He works his way up the aisle to the driver's seat, his hands in the air like he's had enough, which I can't figure because it's me who's just been hurt. "If there's something in there you want, we'll just get it. Ain't nobody locks their doors around here anyways."

I fold up into myself, turning sideways on the seat and

pulling my knees to my chest, and wrap my arms around my legs. This has turned out to be the worst day and I hadn't even got home yet to deal with my dad. "I thought you didn't have no record?" I say. "I thought you weren't no criminal."

Ronnie has started the bus and he's backing it up just a little bit before he turns it onto the road. He looks in the rearview and winks at me and smiles. "I don't got no record, that's true," he says. "What I said was I ain't been caught."

And that's how this happened, me and Ronnie driving down the road to Annette's house after dark in this old clunker he has that's piled up with trash in the back seat. I opened the glove compartment when I got in and out fell a bunch a candy wrappers and all these sets of keys, and Ronnie told me to shove it all back inside and keep it closed. There's a long crack down the center of the windshield and I think to myself that it's liable to break apart if he hits one of these potholes like he does when he's driving the bus. He's more careful in his own car, though, and he talks to me about what we're going to do.

"We'll drive past and if there ain't no lights on, I'll stop and you can run in there and take what you want," he says. "If I was you, I'd go in the mama's room first. Grown women has got more valuables than girls."

He says this and I realize that I don't want anything that belongs to Annette's mother or even Annette and I'm only agreeing to this so that Ronnie won't hurt me again. Him getting rough with me on the bus scared me some. I don't got anyone to go to and even if I told my dad that this man was mean to me, he'd probably tell me I was to blame. Or maybe he wouldn't say anything at all, or maybe he'd go and give Ronnie a beating, but none of that would do a thing for me. So, I'll just run in and take a little something, maybe some lip gloss or a hairbrush, enough to satisfy him, and I surely won't ask to get off the bus again.

"Hope this teaches you a lesson," he says, shaking his head. He's really going on the Skoal here in his own car and he spits some of it out the window, though he doesn't spit far enough and a glob of it lands right on the top of the window that's only up just an inch and oozes down both sides. When he come to get me at the house, he drove up and honked the horn and I don't know where my dad was, so he don't even know I'm gone. Gina still hasn't showed up. I hadn't thought I'd be sad about her, but she was nice to me, most of the time, and she was at least another female to go to. I wonder if I could've told her about Ronnie pinching me, or about going into the Clarks' and enjoying being there and not being sure why. She might've understood what it was like to want to be someplace that feels good.

"I don't need a lesson." I'm hoping against hope that there's a light on at Annette's house, but when we get there to the top of the hill with the hickory tree with the branches that hang out over the road, Ronnie slows down and I can see there's no yellow at the side window by the garage. Behind us is another house, a tall, white one with a truck in the drive, and on the other side of the road is a couple of old barns. "You said that this whole road is her family's," I say. "What if one of them is home?"

Ronnie don't answer and we roll up closer to Annette's, the gravel crunching-crunching under the tires. I can feel the rocks pinging under the car, and I realize that there's a little spot rusted out by my feet where I can see the ground below. Don't anybody take care of nothing? I look up and about jump out of my skin because all the sudden there's a dog up beside us, barking and showing its teeth and acting like it wants to come bust right through the window. I got my window up because there's a chill in the air and I also don't like all that dust coming in on me on these dirt roads, but that dog is right there at the glass and I pull back, scared that he'll get me anyway.

"Shit!" Ronnie swerves the car and I think that's good because if this is Annette's dog or one of her family's, we sure don't want to hit it. That'll only make things worse. But then there's another dog that comes running out of Annette's yard and he joins in with the other one and he's on Ronnie's side of the car. He's a yellow-colored dog with a dark nose and his eyes is wild, and I know there's no way in hell we can get out of this car without one or both of us getting torn apart like a piece of meat. I don't like how this feels, how these dogs are telling me what I already know, which is that I don't got no right to be here. What belongs to Annette is Annette's and not for me to have. I think about my dad saying that if I want fancy things, I'll find a way to get them and maybe that's true, but there's nothing I want here tonight. What I really want is to be on my own—without Ronnie, without my dad—and not living out here where I can't get to nothing without relying on somebody else. But that's not a problem I can solve tonight.

Ronnie's stopped the car and he's rolling up the window as fast as he can so that this second dog won't jump in and grab him, and the car sort of heaves for a second and then goes dead, like it just give up. We're in front of the house now and the long, white fence with hawthorn bushes behind it so full, you can't hardly see through them, but in the dark I see a lamp pop on inside the house and then the porch light and I wish I could hide. Ronnie don't care about hiding, but I can tell that he's in a panic, even though all we've done so far is drive down the road, and he turns the key in the car and it wheezes two, three, four times before the engine fires up and then he's got it in gear and we take off again.

The dogs follow, running so fast it looks to me that their legs could get tangled and I wonder how far they'll keep it up, which turns out to be at the top of the next hill where the road turns and you can't see Annette's house no more. The barking has quit and I look behind us. The dogs are standing in the center of the road, the cloud of yellow dust clearing so that I see them as they lift their noses and sniff the air, satisfied the trespassers are good and gone before they turn around themselves and head back home.

PYRAMID SCHEMES

If she could lose fifty pounds, Tonya would definitely leave Randy. It was no good leaving him now. It was no good being single and fat. She learned that the first time she and Randy divorced. Tonya shifted the car into reverse and started out of the mall parking lot. She'd gone there to buy new bras and panties at Victoria's Secret, but they didn't carry her size and she had to go to Lane Bryant instead. The things she bought there were as pretty and lacy as anything at Victoria's Secret, but she was still disappointed and she went ahead and picked up three new blouses and a skirt to comfort herself. Tonya glanced down at her thighs, noticing the way they pressed out over the beige leather seats. She was even too heavy now for plus-size modeling; this was what the agent at the mall told her. The sign beside the kiosk had said "all ages, all sizes needed." A small crowd of teenage girls gathered to the side, looking at the glossy black-and-white photos of the agency's clients. One of the girls had a line of makeup base at her jaw and Tonya longed to go to her and blend it in with her fingers. The attendant sat beside the kiosk, ignoring the teenagers.

"All ages, all sizes?" Tonya picked up a glossy brochure from the kiosk. "I can't tell you how many people have told me I should be doing modeling."

"Really?" The attendant sat with her legs crossed, delicately balanced on the round surface of the stool. She glanced at Tonya through cat-eye-frame glasses.

"Well, plus-size modeling," Tonya added.

"I'm sure," the attendant said. She smoothed a lock of straight, black hair behind her ear. "But, you know, plus-size models are usually in the size ten to fourteen range."

"Oh." Tonya was starting to sweat at the band beneath her breasts where the underwire dug into her flesh, and she felt the nervous impulse to adjust her bra. "Well, thanks for the information," she said, smiling and straightening her posture. She was wearing her black pumps with the three-inch heels and tried to feel powerful as she turned away.

Tonya watched the teenagers. They had already lost interest in modeling and were headed down to the food court. In all the store windows there were Christmas-themed displays, the dummies dressed in shades of green and red and white. Music from a grand piano cut through the muffled hum of the shoppers. Tonya walked with one foot directly in front of the other, a move that caused her hips to sway. Her mother had told her that was the way movie stars walked, the secret to their elegance. When she was clear of the booth, Tonya whispered under her breath. *Skinny bitch.* It felt good to let the words out even if she spoke them so softly that there was no way the woman could hear her. The whole thing was stupid anyway. How could you be too fat for plus-size modeling?

It was too bad because modeling would've been easy money, which was another thing she needed if she wanted to leave Randy for Donald. Tonya did the math in her head while she drove down the exit onto the four-lane, tallying the costs of living without Randy. Life might be better without him, she thought, tilting her head to the side. Before she could even enjoy it, her teaching salary was gobbled up each month by the mortgage on the house and farm and the payments for her credit cards. Of course, she could always break down and sell Mary Kay or Pampered Chef, but it took a long time to make a profit. The hot thing now was lingerie and sex toys, which she would be great at selling, except that she didn't think she could face her mother if she did it. She was sure her mother wouldn't understand why anyone would want to buy edible body lotion or a vibrator that looked like a tube of lipstick.

She was starting to wish she'd been more careful with the money she made at the supper club meeting she went to a couple of months before. Only about five hundred dollars were left, though she might have put that money in on another club if they hadn't all shut down after the prosecuting attorney in Fayetteville put out word that they were illegal. Randy had told her about it yesterday morning.

She'd just poured a cup of coffee for herself. She blotted her lipstick on the rim and blew across the hot liquid before she took a sip.

"I guess there's been a lot of money changing hands lately," he said. "All the old guys down at the feed store were talking about it."

"Talking about what?"

"Just some deal where you go and give somebody a big chunk of money, then you have to get all these other people to give their money to you." He gulped down the last of his coffee, rinsed the cup in the sink, and left it there. He'd have had to move all of six inches to put the cup in the dishwasher, but, of course, he didn't. "They had a big thing about it in the paper. A bunch of morons throwing money away is what it sounded like to me."

"I hadn't heard about all that." She tried to sound surprised. "I must be living in a bubble."

"Me, too, I guess." He looked at her. She turned her face away and leaned back in her seat at the kitchen table to see into the family room. Jennifer, their daughter, sat on the couch, pushing papers and books into her backpack. Tonya taught at the high school and she'd planned for her and Jennifer to ride to school together that day, but the news about the supper clubs made her want to be alone.

"You know, the bus hasn't come yet," she said to Jennifer. "You can still catch it."

"I'm going on," Randy said from behind Tonya. He walked into the family room and leaned down to Jennifer and kissed her forehead, and she caught his face in her hands and kissed him on the cheek in return. As Randy started for the kitchen door, Tonya thought for a moment he might offer a kiss to her, too. Instead, he reached out as though to touch her hair and then drew it back in a dramatic swoop. "Don't mess it up," he said and, in two long strides, was out the door.

Tonya took the main highway home from the mall, passing the Springdale exit where the Holiday Inn Express was visible from the road. It wasn't true what Randy said about the supper clubs, that it was throwing money away. She hadn't lost anything. In fact, she made eight thousand dollars—more cash than she'd ever touched before in her life—though she'd then gone off and spent a good part of it on things for Donald and their afternoons at the motel. Donald couldn't understand why she insisted they go to the Holiday Inn Express. It would be cheaper to go to the Motel 6 or one of the old motor inns along 71, where no one knew her. But she liked the Holiday Inn Express, where the rooms were decorated in the same tones of beige and pink and green, the towels stacked neatly one on the next in the bathroom, a perfection that could never be matched at home. She never made Donald pay for the room anyway. He'd just started working at the car dealership a few months before and wasn't selling much. Plus, his wife did all the bills and kept track of the checking account. Randy expected Tonya to be a good farm wife and keep the books, but he still checked the bank balance often enough to know they were living close to the bone. He didn't understand where their money went.

"Just the necessities," he'd told her recently. "Until we get ahead a little bit." He had a lot of nerve telling her what she could spend and what she couldn't. She glanced up to look in the rearview mirror and noticed the crease in her forehead just above her nose, and she blamed Randy for it. Now she worried about what he would say when he saw the shopping bag full of new clothes.

Once she turned off the highway onto the dirt road that led to their house, she pulled over by the ditch. She took the bag from the floorboard and folded it over, pressing it flat, and slid it under the passenger seat. The countryside was quiet as she put the car back in drive and started for home, the evidence of her spending hidden safely away. Randy spent just as much and what did they have to show for it? It was warm for the first day of December in Arkansas and the sky was a clear turquoise. She held down the window button on the car door, letting the air rush in. She would sneak out tomorrow morning and get the bag when Randy was feeding his chickens. He was easy enough to fool.

Tonya often thought if Randy would just shut up about the money, she might feel less of a desire to spend it. That was how she'd justified having Donald. She never would've met him in the first place out at the big car lot in Fayetteville if Randy hadn't started in on their finances again, making her want a new car so badly she could hardly stand to look at her old one. Randy closed his eyes and rubbed his forehead when she told him she planned to trade cars that day. "There's no stopping you," he said, not even lifting his eyes to look at her.

"My God, it's not like I'm buying a Mercedes. Anyway, a new car always makes me feel good." She watched him open his mouth, then close it. She imagined he was going to say something about her weight, like if she wanted to feel good about herself, she could spend a little money to join Weight Watchers again and lose a few pounds. He never said it, but surely he wanted to, didn't he? Once, she'd told her mother that Randy was embarrassed by her since she'd become so heavy. It wasn't true, but she was hungry for her mother's sympathy, her assurances that it didn't matter how much weight she put on because she would always be beautiful, no matter what. Now her mother railed against Randy every chance she got. "He ought to treat you better," she said. "If he can't see how gorgeous you are, then you just go find you someone else."

Tonya knew most of the salesmen at the car lot and had taken test drives with two or three of them on days when she'd gone there out of boredom to walk the rows and dream. It was only window-shopping, which in and of itself was harmless enough, but then her attention had turned from cars to salesmen. It was strange how the decision to go to the Holiday Inn Express had come to her like it did with that first salesman and how he didn't laugh or even raise an eyebrow in surprise at her request. Instead, he'd simply smiled and said *yes*. She'd tried to picture herself as it was happening, her body moving down the narrow hall of the motel, an unfamiliar hand at the small of her back guiding her into the room. Her doctor had once given her Valium and she remembered the sensation the drug gave her, one of fearlessness and calm. She'd had the same feeling with the salesman, her arms and legs so weightless and light that her bones might have been hollow as a bird's.

Donald hadn't known anything about Tonya before she'd introduced herself to him that quiet day in October, asking to see every car that was red with two doors. The Honda she was driving then was black, which she'd bought thinking it would make her feel slim and beautiful, but all it really did was absorb heat, making the interior so hot she could hardly breathe. The cars she liked most weren't practical at all for how she and Randy lived. They had a chicken farm ("Poultry operation," Randy always corrected her) and their house sat five miles down a gravel road that wasn't graded very often. She couldn't drive more than ten miles an hour without rocks popping up along the sides of the car and scratching the paint. "That road just rattles a car to death," Randy told her, meaning she should drive a truck, but she refused to do that. Besides, Jennifer loved her cars and begged to ride with her up front. "Daddy's truck smells," she said. Though Jennifer was eight, she was more like a girlfriend than a daughter, so much so that Tonya had nearly slipped and told her about Donald more than once.

But that was what had been so unusual about Donald, that Tonya actually thought about him when he wasn't around, something she tried never to do with Randy. What she had with Donald qualified as a real affair. He was taller than her and thin, with light hair that showed a shiny, pink scalp underneath. He would be bald by the time he was thirty, Tonya was certain, but she didn't mind. She liked him, despite his name. "Donald is not a sexy name," she said one afternoon at the Holiday Inn Express. She lounged on her side, letting the sheet drape over her hip and asked him his middle name.

"Wayne," he said. Tonya felt her heart sink. That was Randy's middle name, too. *Randall Wayne, Randall Wayne, Randall Wayne,* she liked to tease him, saying the names so fast that the "r" came out as a "w." Wayne was the least sexy name in the world.

Donald talked a lot about leaving his wife, Audrey. "You haven't been married very long," Tonya said. "You'd get stuck with child support, but that's about it." When she and Randy got divorced the first time, seven years ago, that was how it had been for them. Her mother and father were shocked when she announced the separation. They'd thought she was happy. *That was before the chickens*, she'd wanted to tell them. Things were better when she and Randy were still raising beef cattle, which Tonya liked because that was what her parents raised and she thought of it as a dignified kind of farming. But before she could realize that Randy was serious about selling off the livestock, he'd done it, and he and his father and brother were busy building long, silver coops down the center of one of their pastures. He sold most of the acreage to pay off old debts left from the beef farm, explaining that poultry was the wave of the future. "Nobody's making a dime off beef now. The smart money's getting into chickens," he said. "Look at Tyson, for Christ's sake."

"All I know is I hate chickens," she told him. "And I hate chicken shit." She never would've said "shit" if Jennifer had been in the room, even though Jennifer was just a baby then. She never would've said it around her parents, either. In truth, she had liked chickens before she had to live on an actual chicken farm. As a girl, she loved the pretty guinea hens her grandmother kept, and she enjoyed gathering up the speckled eggs, carefully placing each one in a galvanized tin bucket lined with an old bath towel. The eggs were still warm when she picked them out of the nests, as though they were alive. But chicken farming was a different situ-

59

ation entirely. Tonya had read an article in the local paper that explained how newcomers to Arkansas sometimes developed a lung condition linked to the poultry industry. They suffered with asthma and bronchitis and a slew of other maladies, but natives to the area were fine, born, it seemed, with lungs immune to the feather and dander particles that lingered in the air. She would like to see the inside of her own lungs, imagining them lined with flakes of soft, white down, quivering with every breath she took.

Not long after the switch to chickens, she had taken Jennifer and moved back in with her parents and filed for a divorce. Before she left, she and Randy had fought mostly about money. He told her she wanted too much, that she wanted everything all at once. "It takes time to build up a good operation," he said over and over. Later, when he asked her why she left, she said she wasn't in love with him anymore, that she'd woken up one day and discovered that the love had disappeared. She watched him put his head in his hands and press at his eyes as she told him she couldn't explain it, but that wasn't the truth. *I don't love you because of the chickens.* It sounded childish, even inside her head, and she suspected there was something more, but the words would not come to her.

"I'd never raise chickens, no matter how damn broke I got," Donald said. He was broke most of the time and upset about money, but not the way Randy so often was. Tonya and Donald had this in common, that they neither one ever felt like they had enough money, certainly not enough to do the things they wanted to do like buy cars and clothes and eat out and not worry about money at all. Donald's parents used to give him extra cash, even after he flunked out at the university and was living with friends and working as a bartender. That was how he met Audrey. She and a group of sorority sisters came in one night and ordered up several pitchers of beer and then got so drunk and wild, he had to help the doormen take them all outside to cool off in the winter air. Audrey's parents had always been generous with her, as well, and he guessed that was why she didn't seem too worried when she found out she was pregnant. His parents were glad when he and Audrey decided to do the right thing and get married, but were surprised when they learned he assumed they would be there to help out with expenses. His father patted him on the shoulder and told him it would be better if he got a real job and stood on his own. "I raised you to be a man," his father told him. Donald said he felt the air go out of him right then, as if his father had punched him in the chest.

Tonya never went to her folks for money, though she complained to her mother that Randy was stingy. She never told about her own secrets, the credit card bills hidden down in the bottom of her purse. She'd rather her mother find out about the men she had sex with at the Holiday Inn Express than about her financial troubles. When Tonya was around her mother, she nearly forgot about it all, the men and the credit cards and the sex. She felt as she had when she was a child, when she did things like show cattle at the county fair and go with her family to the rodeos that came through town every summer. Her brother, Kevin, was a little boy then and her father was young, his hair and eyes shiny and dark, his skin brown from working outside. Years later, after Kevin's accident, her father's hair turned gray and the whiskers on his face went completely white. Until then, everybody said Tonya looked like her father.

It was her father who first told her about the supper clubs, who explained how all she needed was a thousand dollars and she could flip it right around into eight thousand. The whole operation was described in terms of a meal, he'd said, to keep the authorities from catching on. She'd put her money in at the appetizer level, then as more people came in behind her, she'd move up to a salad course, then an entrée, and, at last, a dessert, when she would cash out. No riskier than the stock market, he'd said. It seemed unlike him to get involved in such a thing, but she was flattered he'd included her. The day of his invitation, she went to an ATM and used three different credit cards to come up with the cash, and then told Randy there was a meeting at school and for him to throw a frozen pizza in the oven for himself and Jennifer. The lie didn't bother her at all—she'd just started up with Donald the week before and she felt a rush of invincibility. Donald made her feel lucky.

Cars were parked all over the lawn of the house where the club was meeting. She parked hers alongside several others in an empty cow pasture, and stepped lightly through the high grass and weeds, careful not to snag her pantyhose. Once she got inside the house, the atmosphere was like the church she'd belonged to as a child where people jumped up and down throughout the service, laughing and crying all at the same time, overcome by the Holy Spirit. Everyone in the house was caught up in the frenzy, and Tonya had four or five different people come up and throw their arms around her and tell her that they loved her. "You're the most beautiful thing I ever saw," one old man said, taking her hand to his lips and kissing it. People were sweating and wiping their foreheads on their sleeves, even the women, makeup smearing across their arms. Somehow, Tonya had assumed there would be actual food there, but it was all money, so much cash passing hands that she worried the bills might not be real. She found the organizer in the kitchen and gave him her name, watching him write it inside a square at the bottom of a piece of notebook paper. The man took her thousand dollars and filed it into a yellow envelope on the table. "Don't go nowhere," he said. "We're moving fast tonight."

All the furniture had been moved to the edges of the front room. She took a chair and watched the crowd. They were all strangers to her. Twenty minutes passed while the front door opened and closed, a new stream of gamblers trickling in. The organizer came and sat beside her. "Here it is." He handed her a stack of hundred dollar bills held together with a rubber band. "Eight thousand and no change."

"So what do I need to do now?" She set the money down on her lap, almost afraid to touch it.

"Go spend it, I guess," he said and clucked his tongue. "Easiest money you ever made, I bet."

"I guess it is," she said.

She gathered up her purse and folded the money inside

it and made her way to the door. If she hadn't needed to get home to Jennifer and Randy, she would've gone straight to Donald's house and rung his doorbell and asked him to come out with her, Audrey or no Audrey. But Audrey was a size four ("She's pregnant and she's still a size four?" she had said) and even with eight thousand dollars in her purse, that still made Tonya feel self-conscious. If she were at least down to a size fourteen, she would've done it, no matter what. If she were this rich and thin, too, Randy and Audrey would both be on their own.

When Tonya and Randy raised cattle, they used to go to the farm board meetings together where they would visit with other farmers about things like the price of feed or how much hay they put up that year, how much they might need to buy off other farmers in Kansas and Oklahoma and Nebraska. Her father and mother were at the meetings, too, though they were talking about scaling back and getting ready for Kevin to take over when he was old enough. Tonya sat with her mother and Randy by her father. Her father was a giant next to him. None of them knew all that was to come, that within a year Kevin would be dead, crushed beneath the giant wheels of a tractor and, in another, she and Randy would have a child of their own, the cattle gone and the marriage breaking apart.

The first time she left Randy, she spent hours imagining herself with different men, going to bars and restaurants and taking long weekend trips to Hot Springs or Table Rock Lake. She and Randy never went anywhere because of the farm and it made her feel isolated. Even though she was heavy, she thought of it as a good kind of heavy, most of the weight in her breasts and hips, and she felt confident that she could meet someone new, someone better. "Men like women with a little softness about them," her mother told her.

But none of it turned out the way she'd dreamed it would and she decided part of the problem was Jennifer. It was hard to be sexy when you had a baby, that was what she told herself. Randy called her all the time, asking about Jennifer or checking to see if the child support payment had gone through. He sounded lonely. They had been together since they were teenagers and she wondered why she stayed with him as long as she did, what it was that held them together. "You was just too young, really," her mother said. "You done what a lot of us did, marry the first boy that looked at you twice."

Tonya was in the teacher's lounge one day drinking coffee and wondering if learning to smoke would help curb her appetite when she met Dale Anderson. Dale was a coach and had only been at the high school for a year. He asked her if there was any coffee left. "Enough just for one," she said. Dale stared down the V of her sweater and grinned. Her mother would've been disgusted, but Tonya was happy for the attention and she agreed to meet him that evening at an Italian restaurant in Bentonville. Later, she left her car in the parking lot and went back with him to his apartment. It was in one of the big complexes that seemed to have risen out of the bare fields one spring, a row of honeycombed buildings with no trees or sidewalks, near nothing at all.

Inside, there wasn't much to Dale Anderson's apartment. He had a TV and a recliner and a card table in the kitchen and in his room, a king-size waterbed and a single chest of drawers with another TV perched on top. She'd never been on a waterbed and it instantly made her feel fat. Dale didn't care if she felt fat, though, surprising her with how quickly he moved, how roughly he slid his hands under her clothes and kicked off his own. He fumbled at the thick hooks of her bra. "Goddamn," he said, digging his fingers into the flesh of her back as he worked to get the bra undone. Randy let her undo her bras herself. It had made her angry that he wouldn't try, but as she lay under Dale Anderson, she caught herself missing Randy. When she returned to her parents' house that evening, Jennifer was asleep in her crib. Tonya crawled beneath the sheets of her own bed, not bothering to change out of her clothes or wash off her makeup. She rolled over on her side and stared at the wall, listening to her daughter breathe.

Dale Anderson didn't ask her out again. When she saw him in the hallway at school, she felt herself go hot with humiliation and wanted to hide, all her bravery gone. Soon after that, Randy called, asking if they could get together and talk.

"I think we made a mistake," he told her. "I need to see you."

"I need to see you, too," she said.

Two months later, she married him for the second time while her mother held Jennifer on her lap and her father sat staring down at the floor, the grief of losing Kevin still heavy on him. Randy hadn't taken his eyes off Tonya since she'd said yes to his proposal and she tried to remember why she'd ever left this man in the first place. Chickens or no chickens, this is good, she told herself. This ought to be good enough for anybody.

"I'll have to show you where I live sometime," Donald said one day as they drove around before going to check in at the motel. Tonya had lied to the school secretary, telling her she had a doctor's appointment and couldn't help supervise the cafeteria. She had a preparatory hour after lunch, so she and Donald took their time and made a stop at Sonic. She sipped on a large diet soda while Donald drove. After the incident with the modeling agency at the mall, she'd decided to try to cut back and lose weight.

"I'd like that," she said. "Maybe I can meet Audrey." She gave him a sly grin, tilting her head to the side. She already knew where he and his wife lived and drove past it one day after school. Jennifer had been with her, busy telling her about her own day. Tonya only half-listened as she followed the long, hilly streets that weaved through Fayetteville until she was out into the new subdivisions, areas she knew had been farmland only a few years before. She wondered what Donald would do if he saw her driving by.

"Where are we going?" Jennifer asked, realizing they were nowhere near home.

"I'm just curious about these new houses," Tonya said. "I just want to look around."

"There aren't any trees." Jennifer leaned her forehead

against the window. Tonya wished she wouldn't smudge up the glass that way, but she didn't say anything. Jennifer favored Randy, with her sandy hair and green eyes and pale lashes. Everyone said she had Randy's coloring, but she had not inherited his slender build, which made Tonya sad. She'd watched Randy eat for years, dismayed by how much he could consume and still not gain even an ounce. It wasn't fair to waste such a fast metabolism on a man. When she and Randy were out together, Tonya was certain people thought they were mismatched, like Jack Sprat and his wife.

The houses in Donald's neighborhood were small with oversized garages that pushed out in front and no landscaping other than a few mulch-covered patches dotted with chrysanthemums. She picked his house out from the row and pulled to a stop to look at it from across the street. A young woman came out of the front door and walked toward the mailbox at the end of the drive. Tonya froze for a moment, aware that the woman was Audrey, though she wasn't at all what she had pictured. Audrey's hair was blonde and short, cut in a bob that fell past her chin. She wore a sweatshirt so large it seemed to swallow her up. Donald's shirt, Tonya realized. She wouldn't even be able to fit into one of Donald's shirts. Audrey looked up at her and Tonya panicked, her heart beating so fast, she could feel the blood pulsing in her ears. Audrey waved. Without thinking, Tonya waved back at her and smiled.

"Who's that?" Jennifer scrunched her brows together.

"Nobody." Tonya exhaled and lifted her foot off the brake.

She glanced at Jennifer and then up into the rearview mirror. "Nobody we know."

Donald watched the road as he drove. The dealer car had leather seats and a sunroof. Tonya would insist on a sunroof in her next car, no question about it. "I don't know," he said. "It might be a relief if Audrey knew about you."

"You say that now," Tonya said. "So, do you think old Audrey knows you're up to no good?" She meant to tease him, but Donald was in a serious mood.

He shrugged his shoulders. "You know how you got into that money club thing?" he asked. "I was wondering if there was one still going on that I could jump into."

"Why are you wanting to do that?" She hoped it had something to do with leaving Audrey.

"I'm just needing some money of my own. My bills are eating me alive."

"There's nothing going on right now that I know of."

He shook his head. "I probably don't even have enough cash to put in on it anyway," he said, looking gloomy as he watched the road ahead. When he frowned, his profile resembled Randy's and she wished he would quit.

"You don't need any money if you're the first one up. It's money for nothing as long as you're at the top." She slipped her hand under the strap of the seatbelt that cut across her breast. "Maybe I could just set something up for you myself."

He pulled into the Holiday Inn Express and parked by the side entrance. Her mind was busy now, making lists of people she could persuade to kick in money to a supper club. She almost wanted to tell him to just take her on back to school so she could spend her free hour in her classroom sketching out the plan, but he would be disappointed. "You're something else, you know that?" he said. He leaned in to kiss her and she slid her tongue between his lips. His mouth was still cold from his drink. When she left the car to check them in, she turned to look at him. He was watching her walk, his hands beating out a rhythm on the dashboard.

When she drove home from school that evening, she couldn't stop smiling. "Why are you so happy?" Jennifer asked. Tonya didn't answer. She waved at passing cars, lifting the fingers of one hand so it looked as if she were casting a spell.

"It's weird when you're happy."

"I'm not happy," Tonya said, still smiling.

Jennifer rolled her eyes. This was the first day all week that Tonya had taken her home instead of sending her on the bus. Before Donald, she and Jennifer would take their time going home, sometimes driving up past the Missouri state line to a truck stop where Tonya bought lottery tickets. Along the way were pretty farms with green-velvet fields of alfalfa stretching out across the acres, herds of Black Angus grazing in pastures. One farmhouse she loved the most. It was a clean white with two stories and a broad front porch and balcony, like something you'd see in a magazine, and she had more than once stopped the car at the edge of the property to take it in. Just past it was a dirt road—Dawson Road—where she turned the car around to head back to Arkansas.

Jennifer was silent and Tonya thought again about who all she could bring into the supper club. She knew plenty of people who needed fast money, and if she could get them on board quickly enough, Donald could cash out by the weekend. She pictured him driving up to her house in a dealer car, something shiny and expensive, and leading her away right in front of Randy. She wondered if Randy would say anything, if he would yell at Donald or try to fight him or simply throw up his hands and tell her to go on. Jennifer would probably like Donald, maybe even better than she liked Randy. Didn't girls always side with their mothers?

When they got home, Jennifer trudged out of the car with her book bag slung across one shoulder. Tonya walked with her to the house to unlock the door and then started back toward the car. "Where are you going?" Jennifer asked. "I'm hungry."

"I've just got to make a few calls from my car."

"We have a phone in the house, Mom."

"I need privacy," Tonya said. "I'll be in in a minute." Jennifer was angry at her, but someday, Jennifer would understand everything. Someday, it would all make perfect sense.

It was easier than Tonya thought to recruit supper club members. Clearly, she was wasting her talents as a teacher. She needed to be in real estate or selling cars and making real money for a change. She set out to finish collecting Donald's money on Saturday with Jennifer along in the car. Tonya loved the feel of the crisp hundred dollar bills and she smiled at the idea of lining her bras and panties with them and meeting Donald at the motel. She'd tried all morning to call him on his cell, but he wasn't answering and she figured Audrey had gone into labor. She put her phone on the dash, redialing Donald's number at stoplights.

"You know, Daddy doesn't even have a cell phone," Jennifer said.

"Right, because he works with chickens all day." Earlier, they'd got caught behind a chicken truck. She hated driving behind chicken trucks, but she thought these chickens looked even more miserable than usual, the birds hunched down against their cages for protection from the December wind.

"What's wrong with their necks?" Jennifer had asked. The necks were raw and pink. Bits of white feather swirled behind the trailer like snow. "Try not to look at them, okay?" Tonya said. "Chickens just do that. They're mean to each other for no reason."

She drove through the parking lot of St. Mary's hospital, certain she would see Donald's car there. Jennifer folded her arms over her chest and pretended to sleep. Tonya circled the lot three times. "Let's go on home," she said quietly, pulling back out onto the street.

As she entered the driveway of her house, the phone rang.

"Hey," Donald said.

"Just a second," she told him and motioned to Jennifer with her finger. "Here," she whispered, handing her the keys. "Go on in the house."

Jennifer took the keys her mother held out to her and silently left the car. Tonya watched her go up the front steps.

The wind blew against the girl's back as she worked the key into the lock and went inside.

"So, is it a boy or a girl?" Tonya asked, settling back into her seat.

"A boy."

Randy drove up in his truck and she was scared for a moment, afraid he would come and tap on the window and ask her what she was doing. It was funny how she worried so much about Randy catching her, when, at the same time, she was disappointed when he didn't. He waved at her, his ball cap pulled low over his forehead as he walked on toward the house. He'd always seemed so young, almost like a teenager, but he didn't look young anymore at all. He had creases around his eyes and along his brow, and there was a trace of gray in his blond hair.

"What do you think about it all?" she asked Donald.

"It's all right, I guess," he said. "I held him and Audrey kept asking me the same thing you just did, what I thought about it. I just wasn't wanting all this, I guess."

When Tonya gave birth to Jennifer, Randy stayed with her in the room, insisting it be only the two of them. "Your mother has had the whole nine months," he said. "I at least want this one thing just for us." It was true that her mother had been so involved in planning for this first grandchild that it had seemed as if the baby belonged to her and Tonya, and she cried when she learned she'd have to wait in the hospital lobby until the baby was born. Later, when the room was being cleaned up and Tonya was waiting to be wheeled down to Recovery, one of the nurses took Jennifer from her arms and carried her across the room to Randy. "Daddy's turn," she said in a singsong voice. Randy sat up straight and shaped his arms into a cradle and the nurse placed the baby there. "Wow," she heard him whisper. "Tonya, she's looking at me," he said. "She's looking at me like she knows me."

"Well, you can't always get what you want, Donald," she said, surprising herself with the harshness of her tone. She had taken the money out of the glove compartment and leafed through the bills while she talked. Now, she put the money inside the envelope and slid it into the side pocket of her purse. Randy paused at the door of the house and, opening the screen, turned around. His face was expressionless, but he raised his hand again, two fingers held in a V before he disappeared inside the house.

"Congratulations," she told Donald. "Congratulations on the baby." She ended the call and put the phone in her bag and leaned her head against the seat, her body heavy with exhaustion. She glanced into the rearview mirror and saw the pale line of the road behind her. She took a lipstick out of her purse and ran it along the curve of her lips and pressed them together, blooming the color. When she opened the car door, a cold wind rushed against her, taking away her breath.

Her footsteps crackled across the gravel of the drive. Houses faintly outlined with Christmas lights dotted the horizon, and she squinted, raising a hand above her brow to block her face from the wind. The early winter dark covered the sky so that the first star had become visible. Her father could point out all the planets and constellations, explain the phases of the moon. He'd tried to teach her, too, yet it never made sense. There were too many distractions: satellites and red-flashing radio towers, jet planes full of travelers blinking across the black night. It was too hard to make out what was real and what wasn't. Through the window of the door, she could see the electric flickering of the TV, the shadowed outline of Randy and Jennifer huddled together. They were so close, she could not separate one from the other. Inside her purse, the cell phone buzzed, but she put her hands in her coat pockets and walked to the door.

RETREAT

Dee's hands itched. They itched so much that she was completely miserable, her palms red and irritated from scratching, her fingers puffed up like sausages. The ring she wore on her right hand had become so tight that it felt like her finger might turn purple and fall off. She'd bought the wide silver band with the aquamarine stone last year, when she traded off her wedding set. The only way to ease the swelling was to run her hands under a stream of cold water. But when she got the itching on her hands under control, it would pop up somewhere else—on the inside of her thigh, or between her toes, or even around her crotch, right at the panty line where she couldn't even think about scratching in public without looking completely nasty. When an itching spell came on, it did so with intensity, an intrusiveness that demanded all of her attention, and she could feel the raw sharpness deep under her skin, nearly to her gut.

Still, what caused it? Her mother, Glynn, thought it was the animals, but Dee was unconvinced. The dogs, Ralph and Mickey, were hers to begin with and she'd never had a reaction to them before. The only thing different was they all lived with Gary now—Dee and Ralph and Mickey—and the other animals he kept. "It could be those birds," Glynn said.

"Or that old bobcat. You could be getting bit by mites or fleas or something and not even know it."

Dee rarely touched the animals and Gary was careful to keep them treated for parasites, so what the hell did Glynn know? It was probably a reaction to some chemical, she decided, and changed her soaps and shampoo, stopped wearing perfume, wiped down the interior of her car—the steering wheel, the leather seats, the radio, and the stick shift, anything that she touched. When that didn't work, she considered her job. Could it be all the paper? She hated touching paper, but there was no way to avoid it at Insure-U. Thing was, she'd been touching paper all her life and never had a problem like this.

Maybe, though, it was something outside, like maybe she'd gotten into poison ivy out at Gary's place? His whole yard was a goddamn jungle. Gary liked things natural and he let the yard grow, unrestrained. He didn't believe in cutting back the weeds or putting down herbicide. "I don't want the dogs walking around on all that poison, then sitting down and licking it off," he'd said. "Or Bobbie, either." Bobbie was his first love, a bobcat he claimed to have rescued on a camping trip, bringing her home and training her to use a litter box and sleep at the foot of his bed, where she slapped her fat paw—claws extended—over any leg or hand or foot that dared to stir beneath the sheets. Since moving in, Dee had learned to sleep in one, motionless position: flat on her back with her arm resting above her head.

"Your damn yard gave me something," she told Gary, lying in his bed and digging her fingernails into her palms. The itching subsided when she and Gary made love, when all she felt were his hands and his mouth, the satisfying weight of his body. But once the excitement passed, the threat of the itch returned. "If you cared anything about me, you'd get a lawnmower out there and cut some of that shit down. I bet it's crawling with poison ivy."

"If you'd got into poison ivy, you'd have bumps and blisters, not swelling." He yawned. "I think this itching is psychosomatic."

"What?"

"In your head."

"How could I imagine up anything like this?" She shoved her swollen hands in front of his face.

"Then maybe it's something you ate," he said, pushing her hand away. "Maybe you're allergic to peanut butter. You don't eat meat, so I bet you've been eating too much peanut butter."

"Have you ever seen me eat peanut butter? I hate peanut butter."

"That's weird. Nobody hates peanut butter." He ran his index finger up the center of her spine.

"Half the world hates peanut butter." She reached behind her and slapped his hand away. The itching made her irritable and she felt like punching him in the face. Hitting him would be a release, though she wasn't positive that he wouldn't hit her back. She looked at him as he lay there, his messy brown hair, the stubble of his beard. Gary was a tall, slender man, his body all bone and muscle. He was gentle with her and had never raised a fist or given her reason to fear him, yet there was something treacherous, unknown about him and she was careful not to push.

"Half the world? You got statistical evidence for that?" he asked.

But Dee couldn't take it anymore. It felt like something was crawling on her, like seed ticks or baby spiders. She walked naked to the bathroom, turned the shower on cold, stepped in and let the freezing water fall over her entire body. At first, she couldn't breathe, her muscles clenched tight against the chill, but she made herself stay; if she could stand it a few more seconds, she knew the sensation would change, the itch stopped dead in its tracks. And right when she was about to give in and step out of the water, there it was, the cold not feeling like cold anymore at all, but something akin to warmth. She stood beneath the water, her hands raised up in front of the showerhead, fingers spread out like a frog's, until the itch had been frozen numb. She turned off the water and looked to see her hands were a normal size again, the flesh revealing the bony outline of her knuckles. Her palms were speckled as an egg, white and purple, but the itch was gone. She rubbed her fingers over her face and down her neck, feeling the goose bumps that rose up from her skin. A few seconds more, and she'd be shaking with chills, but for the moment, she felt nothing at all and she savored it.

Gary and Dee were together all the time, at home and at work. Gary was her boss and it was probably bad for the relationship to see each other twenty-four hours a day, seven days a week, but it was better than being on her own. She hadn't liked living alone and it was a relief to have someone to share the expenses again. For the most part, it was fine working with him as long as he did his own thing and let her do the same. On the weekends, he often disappeared for hours, working out on his property before coming back to the house to make supper, occasionally lighting up a corn-cob pipe filled with weed. Dee used to smoke cigarettes, back when she frequented the pick-up bars with her friend, Shelly, but weed made her gag. She preferred beer or a glass of sweet wine. Gary didn't care what she did; it made no difference to him.

What did make a difference to him was how they dealt with Layton, his partner at the insurance office. "I don't want to make it a secret that we're a couple," he told Dee when they first started sleeping together. "But I don't want to broadcast it, either. Layton's real funny about shit, even when it's not his business." Of course, Layton had been gone from the office for most of the summer, at home recovering from a beating. No one really knew what had happened except for what little Layton remembered, that he'd been waiting for a customer in the dark parking lot of an apartment complex in Fayetteville when he was dragged from his car by three men who proceeded to wail on him with baseball bats. When he woke up in the hospital, his wife was there, but so was his father, looming behind her hunched shoulders, solid and imposing as a guard. He'd insisted that Layton come home with him to recover. "If there's more to all this than just an accident, me and your mother will get to the bottom of it," his father announced at the hospital before he spread his hands out over Layton's swollen head and began to pray. It wasn't the first time Layton had been in trouble and there was no point in arguing. After all, his father did hold the title to the business. He'd bought it for Layton after he graduated (a wonder to everyone who knew him), hopeful it would provide the structure his wayward son needed. Layton and Gary couldn't afford to lose Insure-U and the cover it provided for the drugs, so Layton had done as he was told.

But now Layton was back to work, and the office had changed. Gone were the warm, drawn-out afternoons when Gary and Dee entertained themselves by locking the doors and pulling the shades and doing it there in the middle of the office, the fluorescent lights humming above. They'd even returned to driving separate cars to work, though Dee hardly saw the point. Still, it was just as well, since Gary was often out running errands and she hated the idea of being stranded alone with Layton, who'd returned fat and slow and grumpy from his six weeks of recovery at his parents' hands. Gary had warned her, too, that Layton thought he might be responsible for the beating in the parking lot. "That's crazy, though," she said. "You guys are partners. You wouldn't do something like that."

"Of course I wouldn't." He smiled and looked her in the eyes, held her chin in his hand. "Not without a good reason, anyway."

There were plenty of things Dee didn't understand about Insure-U. What she did understand was that Gary and Layton went way back, to when they were new college students living away from home for the first time, smoking together the pot that Gary's father grew on the booby-trapped acres of their house in Gravette. She knew, too, there was money running through the books of Insure-U that didn't come from selling insurance policies at all. They really *did* provide insurance, but only to those who couldn't get it anywhere else, to people with no choice but to pay the heavy fee. The clients were troublesome people—Dee thought they behaved like animals with cars, and it was only Gary who kept her there. When Gary was in charge those six, happy weeks, he conducted the business of Insure-U with so much firmness and authority that she stopped her worrying altogether and, instead, enjoyed the privilege of being the love interest of such an intimidating man. And the money was good, too; Gary saw to that. He gave her a cash bonus every week, which he told her to put back for a rainy day. Dee wasn't a saver, but she did as he said and now had a nice sum of money drawing interest over at the Second Bank of Fayetteville.

"I need to do some adjustments today," Gary told her that morning after they'd let themselves into the office. He disappeared into the kitchenette in the back and returned with a Diet Coke for her and placed it on her desk, then wheeled her in her chair out into the center of the room. "I might make it back for supper tonight, but I doubt it." He gave the chair a hard spin, and she squealed.

"Let's get you going real fast," he said. "Make you dizzy." She pulled her legs in, squeezing her knees up to her chest as the chair slowed to a stop. Her skirt gaped open, showing her panties. She had good legs, she knew, even without a tan, her thighs firm and mostly free of cellulite. Gary looked over at the glass front door, making sure no one was walking by, then kissed her on the mouth.

"When you get home tonight, go ahead and feed Bobbie and the dogs. I'll take care of the birds," he said. "And when Layton gets in, tell him to call me on my cell."

"Can't you just leave him a note or something?"

"Leave it where? His office is a shit hole."

"You could call him."

"True." He wheeled her back to her desk. "But I don't want to. It's part of our dynamic."

"What does that mean?"

He popped open the tab of her Diet Coke, licking the spray off his finger. "It means you just do what I say," he said, bending down and kissing her on the forehead, as though she were a child. "You and Layton both."

Layton never came in at the front of the office, but parked behind the strip mall where Insure-U rented space and let himself in the rear door by the trash bin. Dee tried not to look at him when she heard the door open, though she could hear the rustle of a bag in his hands. Every morning he brought with him a McDonald's bag filled with a dozen biscuits. He ate each one plain, no butter, no jelly, sometimes in a single bite.

"Where's that asshole, Gary?" he asked, a gush of hot air coming in behind him.

"Out," she said. "Adjustments."

"What?"

"I said 'adjustments.'"

"Anybody been in? Any new fuck-heads looking for me?"

"No, Layton," she said, turning her head enough to be heard.

In addition to being fat and ill-tempered, Layton had returned to work paranoid. Each time the office door opened—*bing bong*—his head popped out from his little room. *Turtle Man*, Dee thought every time she saw the bodiless head behind her, his office a giant shell. He'd barely spoken to her before the beating, but now when a customer left, he stood in the back, interrogating her. *Who was that? Did you check the I.D.? Why? Because I fucking need to know, that's why. I'm keeping a list.*

"You're supposed to call Gary," she said. "Catch him on his cell."

"Why the fuck can't he call me?"

"Maybe he doesn't want to disturb you, you know?"

"Fuck that shit," he said. She turned all the way around and faced the front door, hoping Turtle Man would shut up and disappear into his hole. Everything with him was fuck this, fuck that, fucker, fuck, fucked.

It was silent, but when she glanced behind her to check that he was gone, Layton was still there. She felt a prickle shoot up through her jaw, like a needle in her ear, and reached up and scratched it. He spoke. "You and Gary are a thing now."

"What do you mean?"

"You're together, right?"

"I guess so."

"You guess so," he said. "Fuck. That means yes." He slapped his hand against the wall. "You're a happy little couple, just you and Gary. That fucker." Dee didn't know what to say. Was Layton jealous? She couldn't ask him that. If he'd wanted her for himself, he'd never let on. But then maybe it wasn't about wanting her so much as wanting control of Gary? No one controlled Gary, though. Layton had to know that. He turned and went out the door, slamming it behind him.

By noon, Layton had not returned and so Dee locked up as she left for lunch. Her mother had emailed earlier, asking to meet at Chili's. Glynn was a compulsive emailer, sending odd messages throughout the day that hardly made any sense. Dee wished her mother didn't have a computer. They'd stopped speaking for a time after Dee's divorce, when Glynn laid on the guilt, though it was clear she'd been more upset about the loss of property than the breaking of vows. *What about that china? What about all the good stuff people bought you for the wedding? It was worth a fortune and you sold it all at a garage sale!* She claimed to want grandchildren, but that wasn't true. It was only something to say. Now Glynn had her own problems. Her second marriage to a man named Kenny was falling apart and Glynn was on her own again.

She saw her mother's car in the Chili's parking lot and went inside, where the electric blue lights blinded her against the darkness of the bar. Gary refused to go to Chili's; he had too many customers who worked in the kitchen.

"Mama." She touched her mother on the shoulder. From behind, her mother's slim arms and waist made her look like a young woman. It was her face that gave away her age and, somehow, this took Dee by surprise every time she saw her.

"You made it," said Glynn. "I was just sitting here playing with my phone."

"Let's get a table."

"I sort of like the bar here."

"You don't drink."

"I'd sure like to start." Glynn laughed and pointed at the bottles behind the bar. "What tastes like fruit?"

"A daiquiri," said Dee. "Get a strawberry daiquiri. They're sweet."

Her mother confused her. How changed she was from the woman who'd raised her, who'd done everything for her husband and child, even preparing an entirely different supper for each of them, as if she were their servant. Why couldn't they all eat the same thing? It was ridiculous for a woman to live that way. But, still, she should've stayed with Harold, Dee's father, as he'd at least given her some direction. Glynn was someone who needed to be held down, who had to be kept from flying apart.

Glynn got her drink and ordered a barbecued chicken salad and sneered when Dee ordered a veggie burger. "That's why you're so pale," she said. "This not eating meat business."

"It's not that. I'm just not going to the tanning bed anymore. Gary said I looked green."

"Green?"

"Like, khaki," Dee said. "He said you can get a skin infection from the beds. A fungus." She had also stopped frosting her hair and let it return to its natural shade, a dark blonde that Gary said was the color of honey.

"I just started going myself," Glynn said. "I dream I'm on a beach."

"Well, you're just starting things left and right."

"I am," Glynn said. Dee could tell she didn't like the daiquiri. She wanted sweet, but not that sweet. "If I can get this settlement through, I can get me some money, too. Divorce makes you broke. You know what I'm talking about."

"You could get a job."

"I might do that." But she wouldn't. When Glynn was young, she got her high school diploma and then promptly married Dee's father. She'd given birth to Dee less than a year later. The closest she'd come to a job was helping to stage the houses he built and sold. She'd been good at that, making a house look lived in when it was empty as a cave. The houses were poorly constructed and Harold cut too many corners, a scheme that caught up with him in the end. Now he ran a paint store and lived by himself over in Mountain Home.

"What I need to do is get me a Gary." Glynn winked at her. "I like him." She'd eaten all the chicken out of her salad, leaving the greens wilting in the bowl.

"Maybe you should slow down a little."

"You know I eat fast."

"I don't mean that," Dee said. "I mean, just find something else to do with yourself. Men aren't everything."

"Says the one who's never gone without," Glynn shot back. "Like to see you try it. I know all about you."

Dee's shoulders dropped as she felt the crush of the insult. She reminded herself to breathe and took in a deep swallow of air and pulled her shoulders back. The blood flushed from her face into her neck, her chest, her arms and legs, and then she felt a tingle, the beginnings of an itch in the center of her left hand. She curled her fingers down to the palm and began to scratch.

"I shouldn't have said that." Glynn smoothed out her skirt—purple satin, of all things, the hem three full inches above her bare knee. No telling where she bought it. Probably some place meant for teenagers.

"No, you shouldn't have." Her right hand scraped at the palm of her left. She had Benadryl in her purse, but it would make her sleepy and she'd struggle to keep her eyes open for the rest of the day. "I'm not your problem."

"I'm telling you, honey, you got an allergy," Glynn said. "My neck used to turn beet red when I was young and I never did figure what set it off. The doctor said it was a reaction to something in my environment."

"I don't know what it is." She dug into her purse for the Benadryl. She swallowed a pill with a slurp of ice water, wrapping both her hands around the glass for comfort. "Gary says it's in my head."

"You and Gary going to get married?"

"Maybe someday." Actually, Gary had never mentioned getting married and neither had she.

"That'd be nice," said Glynn.

Dee saw her mother squinting her eyes. As long as she could remember, Glynn had been sizing her up. She'd been a doting mother in the beginning, fussing over her, braiding her hair and spraying down the loose strands so she was the only girl in school who never had to pull her hair apart midday and do it up again. By junior high, Glynn had bought her a tool chest full of makeup and wouldn't let her leave the house without lip gloss, as though Dee was a kind of extension of herself. But soon she was no longer an accessory to her mother, but a competitor. If she wore a short skirt, Glynn wore a shorter one; if she invested in golden highlights for her hair, Glynn went platinum. In some ways, they'd even competed for Harold, and Dee had grown up with a feeling of panic, which was only made worse by Harold's indifference. Had Glynn felt it, too? In the end, he'd left them both, smashing up their last house with a sledgehammer, shattering the windows and mirrors and porcelain toilets. He was so far in debt, he needed every penny he could get his hands on, but by the time he managed to sell the wrecked house, there was no profit to be had. In her heart, Dee blamed Glynn for all the troubles. She'd always believed her father to be a good man.

"Listen, Dee, I just want you to know that this divorce has put me in a bad spot. I don't want to ask you for nothing, but I might need to. I don't have nobody else."

"You need money now? Or you just *think* you'll need it?"

"Both, I guess."

"Kenny won't spot you anything?" Glynn shook her head.

The waitress had brought their bill and returned twice to ask if they needed anything more. Dee slid down off the stool. Her panties slipped up her rear, but she wasn't going to pick at them right there in the restaurant. What she needed was some of that new underwear with the little line of silicone along the edges that stuck to the skin. These she had were pretty, but the lace edges slid all over. She'd fix them when she got out in the parking lot.

"Follow me out to my car," she said. "I'll write you a check."

When Dee unlocked the office door, it felt like walking into a refrigerator. It was October, but the heat was nearly as oppressive as it had been in August. Sometimes, she thought about leaving Arkansas, going somewhere north or out west, where there would be more snow. Harold used to call winter "the dead season" because he couldn't keep a construction crew working in the bitter north Arkansas wind. But she had no such worries or concerns, and now she could see winter as a necessary break, a season of retreat.

It was quiet, so she went to the back door and peeked outside. Layton's car was there, so she guessed he was in his office. What did he do in there? The walls of the strip mall were thin as paper—you could hear complete conversations going on in the businesses next door—but Layton had a way of being totally silent and she often suspected he was asleep. He looked exhausted, that was for sure. His wife and three children lived with him in a brick colonial outside of Garfield, just below the Missouri border. They had fifty acres, which his wife needed for her kennels. She was a dog breeder, Gary said.

Dee checked her email—already she had one from Glynn: *will pay you back!! what would I do without you?!*—and then went through the mail. All they had were bills for the electric and phone, which could be put on automatic draft, but both Layton and Gary said no. It was her job to sit down with the company checkbook each month and pay what was due. There were several messages on the phone from customers and one from Gary. He'd stopped by the house while he was out running errands and something was wrong. Bobbie was missing. "She was in the house this morning, right?" he asked on the message. "She always sleeps during the day."

She called him back. "I can't figure this out," said Gary. He didn't bother with hello. "If she's hiding, she's doing a hell of a good job. I can usually hear her purring."

"She's not under a bed or something?"

"We've only got one, Dee," he said. "The dogs are still here and so are the birds and the snakes. Everything's right where I left it, except for the cat. You didn't let her out, did you?"

"I never let her out. That's what the doggy flap is for."

"But she never just takes off."

"You know, Gary, she's a wild animal. She probably comes and goes all the time when we're gone."

"She's not wild anymore," he said. "She's been living inside for a year."

"What about instinct? You're always preaching to me about instinct. Don't you think it applies to Bobbie?" This was true. Gary had a whole philosophy about instinct and survival of the fittest. *We've got to enjoy our evolutionary heritage while it lasts,* he'd said. *One cataclysmic event and we got a total shift in power. The bears or the sharks or the monkeys could take over, for all we know.*

Gary went silent. He was proud of Bobbie, that he'd taken something dangerous and taught it to live with him. The cat had never even scratched him.

"Is Layton there?" he said. "Bastard never called me."

"I'm guessing he's in his office."

"Go knock on the door."

She held the phone down to her side and went back and knocked on Layton's door. No answer. She knocked again, harder, pounding the door six or seven times, and waited. Nothing.

"He's not in there after all," she said. "But his car is here."

"He's off with somebody."

"I didn't think he had friends. None but you, anyway."

"He's got associates," Gary said. "Listen, I'll lock up the house and come on back. I hate to leave, but I need to straighten Layton out on the books. If he comes back, hold him."

Know what I need? A dog!

Glynn was driving Dee crazy. She'd gone quiet again for several days, but now the woman had emailed five times in a single morning. *I need a companion, that's what it is,* she wrote. *I don't like being alone. Nobody does. But I'd like one of those fluffy little white dogs. Like the ones those girls on TV carry around in their purses. It could sleep on my bed. I could take it anywhere!*

They're expensive, Dee wrote back.

Maybe your boss would cut me a deal? Dogs are his side business, right?!

There was no reasoning with Glynn. How did this happen? Dee had called Harold over the weekend, wanting to talk about her mother, but he wouldn't listen. "Bitch ain't my problem," he said, and Dee didn't know how to reply. When she was a girl, Harold served as a deacon in their church, he read the Bible, he didn't allow beer in the house. She'd grown up terrified he would learn the truth about her deceitful heart—the dark, creekside gropings, the things she did to boys in the back of the school bus on field trips. All his strict morality, his righteousness had left him and she found she wanted it back.

She could hear Layton in his office, slamming drawers and talking to himself. If Glynn wanted a dog so bad, she could ask for it herself. The worst he could do was tell her to fuck off. Dee would be the one to pay for the damn dog anyway, but if it bought her some peace, it might be worth it.

Call the office number and I'll put you through to him, she wrote. *Just tell him what you want.*

Two weeks later, the dogs were gone. Mickey disappeared first, and three days after that, Ralph went missing, too. Bobbie had not returned, and Gary stood in the driveway, his arms folded over his chest. "I'm stumped," he said. "They can't be running off. Something's got them."

"Ralph's crazy, though," Dee said. Ralph and Mickey were

golden retrievers mixed with some other unknown, larger breed, their coats more red than blond, their hind legs hunched like a shepherd's. Of the two, Ralph was the more aggressive, far more inclined to resist discipline, though both dogs had been a handful when she and her ex-husband adopted them. Dee took them during the divorce and soon regretted it. They were too much for her, and if Gary hadn't come along, she might've done something awful, maybe dumped them out on a dirt road or taken them to a shelter where they'd have surely been put to sleep. It was cruel, but she'd started to think she would have to choose between the dogs or her life. Gary had saved them and, seemingly in return, the dogs calmed down under his hand. "What could take him on?"

"I don't know." Gary rubbed his head. "Coyotes. A pack a wild dogs. A person."

"Hunters?"

"Hunters. Sure." He sounded doubtful. "I'm thinking I should set up a surveillance camera. Right up there under the rafters." He pointed to the A-line of the roof.

"I can't take this." She waved her hands in front of her. "The bugs are starting to swarm."

There was the smell of fall in the air, the leaves yellowing and beginning to release, but there'd been no killing frost, one that would finish off the insects. When winter came, it would be in a rush, and Gary had gone ahead and stocked up on ice melt and extra cat litter—not only for the litter box, should Bobbie come back, but for throwing under the wheels of his truck if he lost traction getting out of the long, hidden drive. He'd given Dee a bundle of cold weather supplies to keep in her car: blankets, ice scrapers, gloves, and socks, and a pair of cheap snow boots he'd bought at Walmart. In the glove compartment, he placed a two-inch-thick envelope of cash. He was the first man who'd made her prepare for disaster.

"The bugs don't bother me." Gary stared out into the gray woods that surrounded the house. It was sad watching him. He'd been putting out a plate of liver each night, hoping to lure Bobbie home. The liver was gone by morning, but he suspected it was raccoons eating it, not the bobcat. There seemed to be an overpopulation of raccoons and he regretted making the problem worse with the nightly feeding. A week before, one had scratched Mickey across the nose and the blood had poured so thick from the wound, it saturated the fur beneath his jaw, making the dog look like he'd eaten fresh kill.

Bobbie was an intelligent animal in a way that Ralph and Mickey or Glynn's new dog, the little white bichon frise Layton's wife gave her, were not. Since getting the dog, Glynn had come by the office nearly every day to sit in the kitchenette and drink coffee with Layton while he held the dog in his lap. Sometimes, he turned it over on its back and cradled it in his arms, Glynn cooing over the dog as if it were their own child. They sat close enough that their knees touched and Glynn looked at Layton with a dreamy sort of admiration. "You should see him with them kids of his," she told Dee of her trip to Layton's property to pick up the dog. "They're all over him and he stays as calm as can be, twirling them by the arms, those sweet baby dogs yipping and jumping. It's the way family life ought to be."

Layton was probably stoned out of his skull at home, but there seemed little use in telling Glynn. When Dee thanked Layton for not charging her mother for the dog, he shrugged his shoulders and told her it was the runt of the litter and, besides, they had to do something with it. People didn't have the money to buy purebreds like they did before, so it was give it away or take a hammer to its head. She decided not to tell this to Glynn, either, as the dog was a welcome distraction and she didn't want to risk disturbing the calm. Glynn no longer emailed throughout the day or called when this or that odd idea popped into her head. She hadn't even asked for more money. Of course, it was possible her mother had found herself a new man. But wouldn't she have wanted to brag about it? She'd want to make Dee jealous.

Something else had happened, too: the itch was gone. Dee was sleeping well at night and she'd not had a single fit of itching for days. With the exception of the bobcat and the dogs coming up missing and her mother now bringing a new one to the office, nothing was all that different really. But things, it seemed, had leveled out. Even Layton was less moody, more decisive and businesslike than he'd ever been before. In addition to visiting with Glynn, he'd befriended a customer, a younger man, who often came to sit with him in his office, the door closed most of the afternoon. But it was Gary who was the most changed, preoccupied with the missing animals and his search for them. They'd probably just run away, that's what Dee believed. She was sad for

Gary, but not for the animals. Animals could take care of themselves. Maybe she was even glad they were gone, both for them and for herself.

The circle that had surrounded her for so many months, the odd collection of people and creatures, had disbanded, and she felt a particular relief. She should worry about her mother and her new, strange independence, about Gary's pets and even Layton, but it wasn't in her nature. She was no good at caring for so many. At heart, she was a solitary being, at her best when she was alone.

Gary stood beside his car and smoked. The evening sun fell beneath the tree line, the horizon orange as fire. He shut his eyes tight and opened them again, as though he was waking from a dream, then he walked to the storage shed where he took out the lawn mower and began to clear out the tall, dry grass that circled the house. It didn't matter anymore, Dee knew, since the itching was gone and the grass was dead, but it was nice of him all the same. He ran the mower, pushing it up close to the house foundation and under the trees.

The least she could do was put a frozen pizza in the oven for him, maybe tear up a salad to have along with it. Dee peeked out the kitchen window, watching Gary. He stopped and let the engine go off. He'd had his cell phone in his pocket and now he spoke into it, nodding, his left hand raised up to rest on his waist. He turned off the phone and came in the house.

"That was your mother," he said.

"How'd she get your number?" She didn't remember giving it to her, but Glynn could've taken one of Gary's business cards when Dee wasn't watching.

"I didn't ask. She's got car troubles, wants me to come and take a look." He pushed up his sleeves and rubbed his forearms. "I think you gave me your itch."

"She should've called me."

"Nah, what could you do for her?" He scratched at the back of his neck. "I guess she was thinking maybe I could fix it and save her the trouble of calling a tow."

Dee rolled her eyes. "She's supposed to have AAA."

"Too expensive. Said she hit a pothole and heard some kind of *ka-thunk* sound under the car. She's way out by Pea Ridge, near the battlefield."

"What's she doing out there?"

"Driving."

"I figured that much." Dee filled up her cheeks with air and blew it out. She'd just taken the pizza out of the freezer and she turned and put it back in.

"You coming with me?" Gary took his truck keys off the hook beside the door. She scrunched up her face and went to the closet to get her jacket and purse.

Dee had never known her mother to go off and drive for the sake of driving, especially so deep into the country. Still, the directions she gave were good and Gary drove along the twists and turns of Telegraph Road until they were nearly to the Missouri line. The sky was already a dark navy blue, the last streaks of red cloud almost entirely vanished. Glynn had managed to park her car at the entry to a creek, just below a trestle bridge, the old Federal trenches behind them. There were no lights and they didn't see her there until they were only a few feet behind Glynn's car.

"You're a lifesaver," Glynn said when Gary got out of his truck. She threw her arms around his neck, stopping and pulling herself away when she saw Dee. "What are you doing here?"

"You're my mother, not Gary's. You're supposed to be my problem."

"Don't say that." Glynn wrapped her arms across herself as a cold breeze lifted up her hair. The temperature had started to drop. "I just didn't want to bother you with all this. It's crazy enough that I'm here."

"So what's going on with your car?" Gary interrupted, reaching in beneath the steering wheel and popping the hood. "Was it smoking or what?"

"No, not smoking. It just started puttering out on me."

"What are you even doing out here?" Dee was annoyed at her mother. Glynn probably needed to go on some kind of anti-depressant. It seemed like she was slipping.

"I was just out driving," said Glynn. "I'm lonely. Remember?"

"Did you smell anything?" Gary switched on a flashlight and shined it over the engine. "Something sweet, maybe? I had a Ford that always burned antifreeze and it smelled like burning leaves."

"No, nothing like that," said Glynn. Dee watched her mother. Glynn was fidgeting more than usual and she gnawed on the skin of her thumbnail. "I ran over something back a ways," she said. "I heard something hit underneath pretty hard and that's when the trouble started."

"Where's your dog?" Dee asked.

"I left her at home."

"I'll just have to look." Gary slapped his hands against his thighs. "Let me get this tarp out of my truck. Then I can scoot under there better." He climbed into the bed of his truck and took the tarp from the storage chest. He laid the tarp on the ground, pushing it beneath Glynn's car.

"Okay, let's see what we got here," he said from under the car. Dee looked at his legs and his crotch, all that was visible of the man. He looked like something half-eaten. From behind her, there was a rustling sound and a scuffling of feet on the gravel, and as she turned to see what it was, a man pushed her out of the way. She tried to yell, but the words froze in her mouth. At first, she was too scared to see the faces of the men who had come out of the brush, but then she realized one was Layton. With him was the man from the office, the new customer who'd befriended him. Layton and the man screamed as they began swinging with crowbars at Gary's legs, his feet, his crotch, a frenzy of blows, and Dee thought how strange the men sounded, both frightened and excited, like squawking birds. But then it was Gary screaming and calling for help, his voice grated raw with pain. She heard her own name, but she did nothing. She didn't know how to stop the men and she was scared of the crowbars and, for a moment, she felt hot with shame. Then Gary's screams stopped. His legs didn't move at all and even there in the night, Dee could see the darkened stain of fluid spread out from between his legs and across his jeans, something pink and white and grizzled popping up through the denim. She felt dizzy looking at it, understanding it was the white of his bone, busted and ragged, erupting through his skin.

She ran to the truck, but the keys were gone. Where were they? Gary had put them in his pocket. Glynn stood by the ditch, shaking and crying, her hands covering her face. The two men breathed heavy, both of them bent at the waist, exhausted from the work of beating Gary. "Hey, Dee," Layton said, motioning for her to come to him. He covered his mouth with his fist and coughed, spitting out a wad of mucus. "I want to talk to you. Me and Donald here want to talk to you."

She looked around her, at the road and the fields, the bridge up above. She didn't know which way to go. Beneath the car, the light of Gary's flashlight still beamed, pointing toward the creek. "For real, bitch, I'm not gonna fucking hurt you," Layton yelled.

"Dee, it's okay," she heard Glynn say. Somehow, her mother had made her way over to the truck, though Dee had not seen her do it. "Layton won't hurt you. It was just a problem with Gary, okay?" Glynn's voice was soft, comforting, the same as when she talked to her dog. But Glynn wasn't to be trusted; Dee could see that. Her purse was still inside the truck, along with her wallet and house keys and phone. There wasn't time to get them. "He'll help you like he's helping me. We can go now, Dee, we can go," said Glynn.

The other man was collapsed on the ground, lying flat on his back and patting his stomach as though he had simply eaten too much. Layton kicked him in his side, then began to laugh and, at least for the moment, Dee could tell he had forgotten about her. There'd been a house down the road with a car out front. If she ran as fast as she was able, she could make it there. Layton was out of shape, too heavy to run fast enough to catch her. Glynn might try to follow, but she would never last, either. She was too old to get away.

Dee looked over at the car, hoping to see Gary crawl out from beneath it, stand up and tell her he was all right, that he knew exactly what to do. But he didn't stand up and she wasn't sure he was even breathing. A sharp taste of copper rose up from under her tongue and her mouth filled with saliva. She turned and ran. There was no helping Gary without risking herself. He'd made this for himself, hadn't he? And she'd been right there with him. He'd be the first one to tell her to go, to take what opportunity there was to get out. What she had to do was escape, slip into the trees and the dark where no one could see her, no one could follow her steps or figure where she had gone. It all had come down to this, and the best she could do was save herself.

DEEDS

Garnet found the syringes and tourniquet in the ditch by the pasture gate. At first, he thought the length of pink rubber was a hair ribbon and he smiled, thinking of a girl playing near the field, the ribbon falling from her ponytail as she crossed through the weeds. When he knelt to pick it up, though, he saw that it was no ribbon and also that the gate wasn't closed right. In fact, it wasn't closed at all, only propped up against the two young walnut trees that stood on either side of where the posts had been. The posts themselves were flat on the ground, the gray wood busted, the jagged stubs that were hard set in the dirt poking through the grass. The chain and lock dangled off the side of the gate, still connected.

Inside the field were ATV tracks, the lines stretching out like veins across the crushed blades of fescue. The tracks were no surprise. He and his wife heard the motors at night, buzzing along the creek bottom. Even with the line of trees along the bank to filter it, sound traveled for miles across the farm. Garnet's wife, Linda, had grown up there and she could recognize the growl of a car coming from all the way over on the highway. It had taken him a while to become accustomed to it, but he'd learned that if you kept still long enough, all the sounds in the world seemed to drift over the hills and settle into the wide valley. He'd grown up in the Ozarks, too, but on the Arkansas side in a rocky holler so deep, it stayed shaded and dark most of the day, and the silence there was enough to make you think you were the last man left on earth.

Garnet went to the truck and found his cell phone on the seat. He called Linda. "Don't pick it up," she said. "That needle could have diseases."

"I wish I had a plastic bag or something. I've got my work gloves on."

"Leave it for the sheriff. If he even cares to come see."

Garnet didn't put much stock in the sheriff, but he called anyway. The cell reception was better there on the north side of the farm. From the top of the next hill, he could look down over the entire valley and see his own house, the barns and fields around it divided by barbed wire so they made a patchwork of green. He kept the sheriff's number saved on his phone, something he never would've done before, but people were more afraid these days and he guessed he was the same way. The receptionist answered and, rather than put him through to the sheriff himself, she took the message. "We get these calls everyday," she said. Garnet thought she sounded bored. "I give him all the messages and he comes out as he can."

"I wouldn't want a child to get ahold of this needle," he said.

"Are there children just out walking around?"

"There could be." The next farm over belonged to a younger family, one of the few left, but he hoped the mother didn't let her children wander the roads by themselves. There were too many stories.

"I'd just take it and throw it in the trash, it was me," said the receptionist.

"I might. You got my name and number?"

"Yes, sir," she said. "I've got it all down, Mr. Clark."

When Garnet ended the call, he knew he'd wasted his time. Nobody liked the new sheriff, but they hadn't liked the old one, either. It was no honor to be the law. He didn't care one way or the other, but he wished there might be a little help offered on something like this. He hesitated to move the gate and drive into the field, but there were two barns and his own small herd of steers in the next pasture and he needed to check on both. The gate was too heavy to lift now that it was off its hinges and he thought about calling Linda again to see if she might drive over, but Linda wasn't strong like she used to be. Neither was Garnet.

He pushed at the gate to slide it over, digging his heels into the dirt, but it was long and tipped and fell, just missing his feet. Now that it was flat on the ground, he could see the gate was bowed at the center from having been rammed into and driven over. He got down on his knees and shoved it clear of the path. Tomorrow, he'd come fix it, though it would probably be work done in vain. Whoever had been there didn't care about gates or locks, and wouldn't they likely return? He could electrify the whole farm if it weren't for the cost. He had a portable electric fence he moved around to direct his steers to fresh grazing and give them what protection he could. Linda had been angry about the expense of it. "It's not even our farm yet," she'd said, but Garnet thought her objection had more to do with the method than with the money. Her father and grandfather had never used anything more than barbed wire and the threat of their name to shield what they had, and she saw no good reason to change.

It was a dry fall and a haze of dust hovered over the field. Garnet went to the nearest barn first. When he slid the door open, he could tell that no one had been inside. There were no needles, no tourniquets. Not even a beer bottle. He put his boot heel to a rusted tractor seat and gave it a shove, a young black snake revealing itself, hissing as it uncoiled and retreated to a hole in the floor. The second barn was the same, with no evidence of trespassers.

Garnet drove to the creek where the steers had gone to be in the shade and drink. The water at the edge was mossy and the mosquitoes swarmed. He followed the curve of the bed to where it met the branch and there he saw the remnants of a campfire. Beer cans and cigarette butts were scattered beside more syringes, two of them planted needle down into the rocks. He couldn't think of a worse place to have a party than by a creek full of mosquitoes, but it was the seclusion the trespassers wanted. Linda's family, the Dawsons, had lived on the farm for seven generations and she told him that the first ancestors who settled there had passed on stories of how frightened they were at night in the isolated Missouri wilderness. Indians lived on the land then, too, and they camped on the creek bank where they sang and hollered late into the night, their bonfires burning until morning. "Wouldn't that like to have scared you to death?" she'd said. "I don't know how them old people hardly stood it."

Though he'd nodded in agreement, he didn't feel sorry for the Dawsons. You moved into somebody's territory, you had to deal with the consequences. Maybe the Indians were just trying to scare off them and the other white people, maybe they were just trying to give them fair warning? Linda's family had been the intruders, but those days were gone and the Dawsons were the natives now. He looked closer at the blackened rocks surrounding the campfire. There used to be arrowheads all along the creek, but they'd been picked clean by people who snuck down and filled their pockets with relics. Still others came at night to hunt game, shining their flashlights into the trees to catch the mirrored eyes of coons and possums. If it wasn't one thing being stolen, it was another, and you could never let your guard down.

Garnet walked back to the truck. Three of his steers had gone off somewhere on their own and he needed to find them. He turned the truck around on the gravel bank and headed to the neighboring pasture.

The next morning, Garnet set to work welding a disc on the hay mower. Linda's brother, Jody, had run it over a hunk of rock and knocked off a blade. This was the way of it: Jody broke things and Garnet put them back together. He wouldn't have bothered with it right then except the late drought had left just enough grass for a final cutting of straw, which he needed for the animal shelters in the winter. He lifted the faceplate. Was somebody calling? He wiped his face on his sleeve and stuck his head outside the door of the shop. It was Linda yelling for him from the back porch. She waved the phone in front of her.

"It's the sheriff calling you back."

He took off the helmet and left it on the floor of the shop. He hadn't expected to hear from the sheriff and now he wasn't sure he really wanted to talk to him.

Garnet was breathless by the time he made it up the steps of the house and his fingers were too greasy to be touching the phone. Linda saw his hands and grimaced, but gave him the phone anyway.

"Yes, sir," he said into the receiver.

"Got a message here you found some interesting items on your land."

"I guess that's what you could say," said Garnet. "A bunch of needles and such. There was more at the creek. Guess somebody was having a party."

"It wasn't the vet might've left it all?"

"No, sir, I hadn't had the vet out since winter. And she don't usually hang around and make a bonfire." He could see already it was no good talking to the man.

"You got 'no trespassing' signs along your property?"

"I do. Now this over across the creek is my father-in-law's place, but I keep the signs up for him."

"So you're calling me about somebody trespassing on land that isn't even yours?"

It was hard to explain the situation with the land, and it embarrassed Garnet to be put on the spot. Linda's father,

Leland, was in his eighties, but he refused to sign over the deeds. A sensible man would've done it twenty or thirty years ago, when his son and daughter were still young enough to make a go of the farm, but not Leland. He'd moved into town with his new wife, a sour-faced woman who thought she'd like farming until she learned how quiet and lonely it was. She said they were too old to live so far from a doctor's office and, since the move, Leland had proven her right, becoming too feeble in mind and body to even drive himself the twelve miles out to the farm to check on it. In his final years farming, though, he hadn't taken good care of the place. The job of replacing the collapsed fences and reclaiming the land from the overgrowth of thistle and thorn trees had fallen to Garnet, now in his own retirement, and as he made his way through the neglected acres, he came across strange things. In a forgotten silo pit, he found the Dawsons' old mailbox, painted by Linda's mother, Ivy, with a morning glory vining in and out of the family name, a busted headboard thrown in on top of it. A burned-out oven had been tumbled into a cluster of trees just inches above the creek's edge, a refrigerator not too far from it. In his old age, Leland had used the farm as his personal junkyard, a change from the neat and prideful man he'd once been.

Still, when the subject of the deeds came up, Leland returned to himself, huffing and sputtering that the land was all he had left, and he might need the money from its sale for his own survival. He'd inherited it from his father, whose other sons had died in their youth, killed by disease or war, and Leland took it over early in his marriage to Ivy. But he'd forgotten about his father, the vastness of his gift. "Wasn't nobody ever helped me with nothing," he'd said. "I built that farm on my own."

"I'm sort of the land manager," said Garnet. He hoped that would be good enough for the sheriff. "I take care of the place for my father-in-law. He can't do it hisself. You know Leland Dawson?"

"I know the Dawsons." There was a coolness on the phone that took Garnet back. Used to be the mention of Leland's name made doing business easier, but he supposed the old man's power had faded with age.

"Just keep track of anything else you find. And if you actually catch a body there, call me," said the sheriff. "Until then, I'll just worry about these murderers and rapists I got running around here, if that's all right with you."

Garnet was angry when he hung up. "I see why people say what they do about that one," he said. Linda had stood right there during the entire conversation, and he knew she'd heard it all.

"You shouldn't have let him talk to you like that," she said.

"What was I supposed to do?"

"I don't know."

"Then don't tell me I done something wrong." He got a glass of water and drank it in hard gulps.

"I didn't mean it like that," said Linda. "But you'd think a sheriff would care more about what all went on."

"The country's full of criminals. I guess our troubles aren't too special." It was true that the countryside was infested with people cooking meth and doing things you'd think would only happen on TV. When their girls were growing up, it was marijuana that was everywhere and the state police helicopters flew over nearly every night, infrared lights blinking like UFOs. It was a nuisance, but there hadn't been so much violence as now. A month before, a man killed his girlfriend's child, cutting the boy's throat from ear to ear, the man then taking a picture of it with his phone and texting it to his own mother to ask her what to do next. Before that, a group of students from the college in Rolla were doing a river cleanup along the Big Piney when one of them saw what looked like the top of a smooth, white rock. It turned out to be the skull of a man who'd gone missing a year before, the rest of his bones soon found in a nearby field. His father and brother confessed to the crime, explaining the murder was an accident, though why they separated the head from the body had remained unclear. Southern Missouri was a hard place, but it was less so before the jobs disappeared, the shoe factories sent to China and the little businesses gutted by the giant stores built along the highways and interstates. It had become a land of old people. No one's children came back after they left, no one wanted to farm and live where everybody was so poor. Garnet's daughters were the same way and he knew they'd never come home for anything more than a visit.

"We'll just have to keep an eye on things ourselves," Garnet said. "I'll talk to Jody about it."

"I already did," said Linda. "But I bet he'd want to hear

about this sheriff. He's said all along he wasn't good for nothing."

Garnet took the mower out and tested it in the field. It worked fine and he considered going ahead and cutting the tall grass, but he stopped when he saw Jody coming down the road. Jody had moved into the old farmhouse when Leland left for town, promising to maintain it and help with the land, though, so far, he'd done little. He'd spent most of his life working at the dairy plant in town before it closed its doors and left him with nothing to do. Garnet had worked away from the farm, too, spending weeks at a time in the dark engine room of a towboat on the Mississippi River. It was a good job—better paying than anything at home—and he'd felt his girls and Linda were safe living without him there among the Dawsons.

Dust flew out around Jody's blue truck so that it traveled in a pink cloud. He stopped and stuck his head out the window. "Ain't you about on fire?" he said. "You need a canopy on that tractor."

"I know it," said Garnet. "Maybe I'll wait 'til morning on this."

"If you wouldn't mind, I could use that field down there by the cemetery cut, too."

"Well." Garnet got along with Jody well enough until he did things like this. Overweight and in declining health, Jody liked to talk farming more than actually do it. Linda said he'd always been lazy, even as a child. "I'd have to see if this mower holds up."

"The old man left us a whole lot of junk, didn't he?" Garnet didn't want to get pulled into a conversation about Leland. Jody'd get a person to say things, then he'd go and repeat what was said.

"Linda told you what I found across the creek?"

"Yeah, she did," said Jody. "Burns me up thinking about people creeping around like that." He patted his shirt pocket and found a cigarette to light up.

"There's always been trespassers. But this is something different altogether."

"Yeah." Jody took a long draw on his cigarette, blew the smoke out his nose. "Not sure what to do about it, short of running razor wire all around the place."

"I'd about do it if it would keep the deer hunters out, too."

"God, yes," said Jody. "Them damn bow hunters is already started."

Last fall, Garnet had been moving hay bales over by the Gaddis place when he heard a rustling not more than fifty yards away. A doe fell, he saw it then, and a hunter, covered head to toe in fancy camouflage, came out from the trees, pumping his bow over his head like a trophy. Garnet watched as the man knelt in front of the doe and ran his knife along its belly and up along its hind legs. He cut the loins from it, folding the bloody meat into a giant ziploc bag he pulled from his vest. He stood then and made for the road, the slain animal left in the thinning shade of a hickory. When he noticed Garnet was watching him, he spoke. "A little something for the coyotes," the man said, pleased as if he were doing the world a service. Garnet didn't hunt.

He'd had his fill as a boy when he and his father had to do it to put meat on the family table. It was a daily task for them and they wore their regular clothes out in the woods. Animals knew you by your sounds, by your scent. They couldn't be fooled by how you dressed. Garnet's father would've mocked these men in their special hunting clothes, even their boots covered in splotches of green and brown and gray. To Garnet, the way they tried to hide themselves, to blend into the trees and brush, felt like cheating.

"Linda said you got an opinion on this sheriff."

Jody rolled his eyes. "He's that Darren Moseley. Went to school with him until we was juniors in high school. His family moved off away somewhere. Memphis maybe," he said. "Too bad he had to come back. He was always running his mouth. I remember when we was in elementary, he threw all my books out the bus window. The driver had to go back and pick it all up and when he got hold of Darren, he whipped him good. You never heard a kid howl like old Darren did." Jody smiled at the memory and flicked the ashy end of his cigarette down the outside of his truck door.

"I don't know what I think of him," said Garnet.

"I know what I think. He's an asshole."

Garnet looked behind him at the tractor. He'd probably made himself trouble with the sheriff, but maybe it wouldn't matter.

"Let me know if you think you can cut my field," said Jody. He never stayed interested in a conversation not about him for too long. "I'll open the gates." He threw out the end of his cigarette, which landed in a ditch full of dried grass.

Garnet waited until Jody drove off before he slipped between the lines of barbed wire and ground the butt into the dirt, smothering what fire it had left before it could catch.

On Sunday, Garnet and Linda went to church. They used to go to the little Baptist church near the farm, but hardly anyone went there these days. Garnet had been relieved when Linda said she was ready to leave it, too. They joined up with the Methodists in town, a dwindling congregation, but one where your personal business was your own, and for the first time in his life, Garnet enjoyed getting up on Sunday morning.

When they were finished at church, Garnet asked to stop at Leland's house. "I'd rather not, but I guess we have to," said Linda.

"Maybe Edna won't be there," he said. Edna was Leland's new wife.

"She'll be there." Linda pressed her fingertips into the place between her brows. "But I know you need to get that check."

"If I wait, he's liable to forget about it or tell me he done paid me already." Garnet had put in his order for fertilizer for the following spring. It was like with the gas man: if you paid for it early, you got a discount. He and Linda took care of the land and kept the money they made running steers, but Leland was supposed to pay half on the fertilizer since he took the money from the excess hay they sold. It was a deal that tilted in Leland's favor, yet he had a way of making Garnet feel like a beggar when it came time to get his check.

"Maybe we'll catch him in a good mood." Garnet parked their car in front of the house and they walked up the drive to the side door. Leland and Edna kept the front door locked, a heavy china hutch pushed in front of it on the inside. The side door, though, was kept unlocked, and Linda knocked before she opened it an inch and called inside to announce them. Edna was in the kitchen and she came to the door. "You can come in," she said. She never smiled at Linda or Garnet, and she turned her back to them and went down the dark hallway. She called to Leland. "You got visitors."

Leland came out of the back room. When he walked it was with his shoulders hunched over and he scuffled his feet against the carpeting. Garnet had never realized how small Leland was until recently. When he was younger, Leland was solid and strong and wore cowboy boots with two-inch heels, a favorite gray Stetson hat with a scaled, silver band. His black hair hadn't faded a bit until he was into his seventies. Leland acted like a tall man and Garnet had believed he was.

"How are you today?" Garnet sat down on the couch next to Linda and he reached out his hand to Leland. The older man's handshake was weak. "Been working hard?"

"I got my garden cleaned up," said Leland. "That about put me under."

"I'll bet. This heat like it is. The seasons done got all mixed up." He wished Linda would help make conversation, but sometimes it felt as if she was the in-law in the room rather than the blood daughter. It had been like that since Ivy died. Leland shifted in his seat and crossed his arms over his chest.

"I heard you called the sheriff this week," said Leland. "Told him I had drugs on my place."

"Well, no." Garnet felt his face turn hot. "I told him I found things left by some people that was trespassing. They was doing drugs over there. I never said you had anything to do with it."

Edna came out from the kitchen. "You know he gets upset," she said. "You know he don't like gossip."

"Who'd you hear all this from anyway?" Linda asked her father. She wouldn't talk to Edna unless she had to. Five years had passed since Leland's remarriage, which had taken place less than three months after Ivy's death. Linda said there were other women she could've accepted, but not Edna Wilhite. "He'd have never even spoke to a Wilhite when Mom was alive," Linda had said. "A Wilhite boy asked me out once in high school and Dad threw a fit. Said the Wilhites wasn't fit to slop hogs, let alone court a Dawson. Guess he forgot about that."

"I'm not gonna tell you who told me," said Leland.

"You don't have to," said Linda. "It was Jody, bet you anything."

Leland pursed his lips together and started to shake. "It don't matter who told me, but I'm telling you both right now that I don't want that damn sheriff out there on my land. No telling what he'll pin on me. I've heard what he's like."

"I won't let him out there," Garnet said. He felt shamed. There was no talking sense to Leland. The old man had grown fearful of others, often believing that his money had been stolen straight out of his bank account or that he was receiving threatening phone calls. Edna said the calls were from politicians and businesses, recordings that started playing the minute you picked up and wouldn't stop no matter what you said. Leland needed to go to a home, but Edna said it would eat up all their money. It bothered Garnet how she called it "their money" when she'd not been the one to earn it.

"I pre-paid the fertilizer man," he said. Like with Jody, it was often best to change the subject and, besides, if he didn't get it in soon, Leland would shoo them out the door and he'd have to try again later.

"How high was it this year?"

"About the same as last, so not too bad. We're going halves?"

Leland let out a long breath through his nose. "I guess we are." He was still upset about the sheriff. At his knees was the coffee table and he reached down and pulled open a drawer and took out a checkbook and a pen. He looked over the old entries. "I paid you five thousand last year."

"You did. That'll be fine for this year, too."

Leland paused before he wrote in the numbers, circling his pen above the paper like he couldn't decide what to do. He wrote out the check and folded it in half and handed it to Linda. "I reckon you two want to get home."

He was mad and wanted them to leave. Linda and Garnet got up and went out the side door, Edna following them to shut it all the way after they were gone. In the car, Garnet started the engine and pulled onto the quiet street and headed north toward the farm. They knew not to look at a check in Leland's presence, and Linda waited until they were even out of sight of the house before she unfolded it. She let out a light gasp and when Garnet looked at her, he could see her eyes rimming red.

"He couldn't be that mixed up." Linda had stopped crying, but she'd been so keyed up pulling off her pantyhose, she'd put her thumb right through the nylon. She threw them on the floor and found a pair of shorts to put on. "He sat right there and made it out for a thousand. Bet Edna had herself a good laugh when we was gone."

Garnet didn't know what to say. He'd never thought of Leland as one to swindle on a deal, but with Edna, he'd become a man to watch. The spring before, loggers had shown up on the property, there to cut down the walnut trees. Garnet tried to send them away, telling them they were at the wrong place, but the man driving the truck said, "Mr. Dawson hired us." He let them in, but hated it. Every fall, his grandchildren picked the black walnuts, their limey-scented hulls staining their clothes, and sold them for cash. Leland had told the loggers they could take as many trees as they could haul and the money was to go to him. He'd done the same with the creek gravel, sending a dump truck from the concrete business in town to the creek to scoop rocks and sand out of the bottom and along the banks, nearly ruining both.

The dog started to howl and Linda lifted the curtain. "Jody's out front." She picked up the ruined pantyhose and threw them in the trash.

"Sure wish I could have a single day that I didn't have him standing at my door."

"Don't tell him about Dad shorting you."

"I won't."

"He'll just make it worse."

"I said I wasn't telling him."

Garnet had changed into his work clothes and buckled his belt as he went down the hall to the living room to open the door. The dog was still howling, but stood off in the corner of the porch.

"You need to get rid of that dog," said Jody. "He's gonna hurt somebody."

"He's just guarding his house, doing what he's supposed to do. What can I help you with?"

Jody looked over at the dog and hissed. His t-shirt and sweatpants were spotted with oil stains. He was a childish man, in his ways and in his dress. Garnet didn't know how he could stand to walk through brush out in the field in those sweatpants. Surely he was covered with the prickles of beggar's lice and cut through from thorns by the time he was done.

"I need you to come over across the creek with me."

"You got a steer loose?"

"Nah," said Jody. "Problem with my fences."

Garnet's work boots were down in the basement. "I'll meet you round front," he said.

Jody went back to the little ATV he used to drive around the farm. When he first bought it, he told everyone that he'd bought a mule. "I'm going back to the old ways," he said as he tried to hold back a smile. It turned out to be a Kawasaki, a model called a Mule, but larger than the ones people rode for sport, and it had a small truck bed on the back for hauling things. He drove the ATV too fast up and down the dirt roads and he'd flipped it over on himself in the first week, but somehow managed to not get hurt. Garnet thought it was a toy for Jody, one more thing for him to play on.

When Garnet got in the ATV, Jody revved up the engine and pulled onto the road and sped down to the big gate near what had once been the milk barn lot. He drove the rutted path into the creek valley, where the trees shaded the water. The wheels spun in the sandy dirt at the edge of the creek, but then caught purchase and they crossed over the low water.

"Where you going?" Garnet had to shout to be heard above the sound of the motor.

"Over yonder." Jody pointed to his left.

"The woods?"

Garnet hadn't been in the north woods for a long time. It was where some of the early family was buried, along with their few slaves, but no one was sure where. The headstones had disappeared.

"I found something over here." Jody stopped the ATV and got out. Leland had never wanted cattle in the woods, and the area was sectioned off with a long fencerow of barbed wire. Jody pushed a wire down to make room to climb through, but one of the barbs caught on the seat of his sweatpants and he started to cuss. Garnet went to him and unhooked him before crawling through himself.

The woods were as dark as he remembered, thick with black walnuts, their leaves already half gone. Why hadn't Leland told the loggers to cut these down, too? He supposed it was because there was no gate, no easy access, and to get in would mean cutting fences.

"Here it is." Jody was panting from the short walk and he let out a cough from deep in his chest.

"Here's what?"

"This is why we've had visitors." Scattered along the ground was a variety of bottles, cleaners and chemicals Garnet recognized from his days working in the engine room of the towboat. There was a propane tank and several beaten-looking pans. A sharp odor rose up from the ground. "They're cooking meth back here," said Jody. "I'm surprised they ain't burned these woods down yet."

"Whose is it, you think?"

Jody looked at Garnet and raised an eyebrow, then turned and spat a line of chew off behind him. He slurped at his lip. "It's that grandson of Edna's," he said. "How much you think this shit sells for?"

"Enough to buy a man some prison time, I'd imagine. You call the sheriff?"

The spot in the woods was covered over in branches so thick, Garnet could barely see the blue of the sky. When he looked up, he caught just the glimpse of a jet plane going over, trailing a thin, white line of exhaust. He'd loved looking at the sky over the Dawson farm, the way it met the rolling green of the hills in spring and summer, the dry grass in autumn and then the snow in the winter. The farm of his childhood was bleak in comparison, and he'd coveted what Leland had.

"I'm not sure calling the sheriff is the best thing, Garnet." Jody hardly ever called him by his name, usually beginning his requests with "hey," instead. "I've been thinking about this and I know you know how Dad feels about having the law out on his place."

"I'd think he wouldn't want nothing like this on it, either."

"If he'd even know what it was." The dappled light of the woods fell across Jody's shoulders and chest and then disappeared. The few clouds overhead moved across the sun and the woods felt cooler and darker. "It's occurred to me that Dad might not have the money he used to have. Edna's bunch never had two dimes to rub together and to hear the gossip, she's milking the old man dry. Might be we need to make the most of this."

Jody had worn his black cowboy hat, which was another thing about him that Garnet usually found silly, but this time, it was different. Jody pushed the brim low on his forehead, his eyes barely visible. The hat was unnecessary in the woods and he could've left it in the ATV, but now he seemed to be hiding under it. He took the can of snuff from the right pocket of his sweatpants and tucked a pinch in his bottom lip. The nubs of his teeth looked like those of an armadillo. They were the only animals Garnet bothered to shoot and he did so because of the mess they made of the pasture, the holes they dug a danger to the cattle.

"I'm calling that Sheriff Moseley," he said. He made to go back to the ATV and get home, a feeling of urgency moving inside him. "I know there's bad feelings between you two, but he's the only law we got. I can't let these people stay here. They'll hurt us."

"Listen," said Jody. "I already dealt with Darren, but I'm just going to tell you something else straight out. You don't got a voice in this. You're not a Dawson. This is Dawson land, not Clark land. And I'm the only Dawson here. I'm the only one who's got a say."

"I'm married to a Dawson."

"That don't count. She's a Clark now. Like you."

"She's set to inherit her two hundred acres, though, like you," Garnet said. "These woods right here is a part of that." If they didn't get rid of the trespassers now, wouldn't it only get worse? Wouldn't there be more following behind them? But Jody didn't care about people coming and going on the land as long as he could profit from it. Garnet thought of the hunter taking the loin from the doe, leaving behind the carcass. He had despised the wastefulness of the act, but it was the hunter's sense of privilege that most angered him. The man was not a predator so much as a parasite—taking only what he wanted and leaving the rest—and Garnet could see that Jody was the same.

Jody took off his hat and pushed back his hair, slick from oil and sweat. "Don't be so sure of that. Me and Dad's been making some changes."

Me and Dad. Garnet remembered what his mother-in-law had said about Jody once. It was just the two of them, Garnet and Ivy, with no one else around to hear what was said. They often talked when Linda and Leland were gone, and there was a kinship there, the two of them both having come from somewhere else to live with the Dawsons. "I should've drowned him as soon as he was born," Ivy said. Jody had been causing trouble and he fought everyone who ever loved him: his wives, his sons, his mother and father. Everyone had to do exactly what he said or he'd blow up, starting wars that could go on for years. That was why he worked at the milk plant instead of with his father on the farm, because he couldn't get along. Ivy and Leland stood by their son, but there was little reward for their loyalty. Garnet wondered if it had been Leland who was so committed to Jody's welfare, if Ivy would've been just as satisfied to let him go.

"I guess I need to ask you what that means," he said. His jaw was stiff and his heart was pumping hard in his chest. "But I figure I already know."

"He just wants me to be set up with the best land, being the only son and all. These woods is worth a fortune, but this little drug business is something, too," he said. "I've always wished I'd had the nerve to get in on that pot business, but this might be better. I talked to this boy of Edna's and he knows he can't be out here without kicking something back to me for letting it stand. He forgets to do it and I'm calling in them loggers again."

Garnet stood back and regarded Jody.

"Is Leland signing over the deeds to you then, if you're so fired up to get in on this mess?"

"No, he's not." Jody grinned. "But that's what's so good. There's any trouble, I pin it on the old man, right?"

"Even if the trouble's right behind your own sister's house."

"Shit." Jody shook his head. "You're a hard-headed son of a bitch, you know that?"

"If this is how it's going to be, we want whatever land is coming to us now. We'll sell and get the damn hell out."

"He won't do it." Jody wiped his mouth, saliva oozing from the edges of his lips. "It wouldn't be fair. If he won't deed to me then he won't deed to Linda, either. He's real big on fairness." He spit one last time, a trickle falling in a brown drop on his chin he caught with his thumb. "And he's scared. Afraid he won't have nothing. Sometimes, you just got to take what you can get."

Garnet turned to leave, slipping back between the barbed wire. He wouldn't ride in the ATV. It was a long way up to the house on foot, but he wasn't like Jody, who could hardly hike himself up the front steps of the farmhouse without having a heart attack.

"Where you think you're going? You'll get snakebit out in that field."

Garnet kept walking. There was an eagle's nest at the edge of the creek and he'd seen it and its mate hunting when he was over here on the north side. Last spring, he'd seen one of the birds flying through the air, the writhing body of a small animal dangling in its claws. The nest was as big as a bathtub and the eagles had spent two full years building it. If no one bothered the birds, they would stay there the rest of their lives.

Garnet heard Jody curse him—*fucker*—then start up the ATV's engine.

The Mule growled past him, Jody revving the engine to show off. For a second, the front wheels came up off the ground and Garnet thought the ATV might flip over. He pictured Jody's neck snapping in two. Life would be easier if he was gone, but it seemed he was set to hold on, at least for the time being.

Tomorrow, Garnet would go to the farm supply in Monett and get the rigging for more electric fencing and he'd stretch it as far as he could to keep his cattle and pastures separate and safe. He could do what the marijuana farmers used to do, booby trap the fields, hang hooks at eye level from fishing line—the tricks his generation of soldiers learned in Vietnam. He could string them between the trees at the edges of the pasture. Sure as anything, Jody would be the first one to run through the trap and get his eyes torn up and Leland would throw Garnet off the land. But it would please him, wouldn't it, to hurt Jody? To scare Leland? To make father and son fear the place they thought they knew so well?

Garnet heard the splash of the ATV's wheels in the creek water, the grinding of tires into gravel, the motor giving off a high-pitched squeal. Jody was probably spinning at the slope that led up out of the creek bottom through the pathway of trees. It wasn't the engine that was the problem, but the tires. Jody never replaced them and the treads were worn nearly bald. If he wasn't careful, he would slide right back down the incline and have to leave the ATV there in the creek. Then he'd come ask to borrow Garnet's tractor to pull it out and act like nothing was wrong between them.

Jody was yelling. Garnet walked up to the ridge between the field and the creek and saw him there behind the ATV, leaning and shoving against the tailgate. His feet were too swollen to wear work boots and he stood in the shallow water in his white tennis shoes. The water had siphoned up his sweatpants so that they were heavy, pulling down, and part of his ass was showing. Garnet pretended he didn't hear or see anything, but then he realized that the engine was still running as Jody pushed, his feet slipping beneath him.

He neared the creek, waving his arms in warning, though Jody was turned around and couldn't see him. "Turn that engine off." He called out as loud as he could, but it made no difference. He wondered if Linda could hear them at the house.

Jody looked over his shoulder. If he saw Garnet coming, he didn't seem to care. He pushed at the ATV again and it slipped forward suddenly enough that he lost his footing in the muck and landed on his knees. He used the bumper as support to pull himself up, but the ATV gave way again, backwards this time. Jody's face knocked against the tailgate, throwing his head back as if he had been punched under the chin. He fell under the body of the vehicle.

Garnet heard the sound of his own breath suck into his throat as he watched Jody fall, felt the hard dirt under his boots turn to gravel as he ran to the creek.

The hit had knocked Jody unconscious. Garnet reached

into the ATV and turned it off before he went back and squatted in the water beside his brother-in-law. Jody was too heavy to lift and he was afraid to move him anyway. Beneath the Mule, Jody's legs were bent backward below the knee, his back oddly twisted and arched. The water, though, was too shallow for him to drown.

Garnet had left his cell phone at the house, but it wouldn't have done any good. There was no signal in the valley. He'd have to run home to call 911. After that, it would take an hour for the ambulance to arrive and even then it wouldn't be able to make it down the rough, steep path to the creek.

There was no reason to rush. A breeze swept over the water, a welcome coolness in the heat. He stood up and cupped his hands around his mouth and called out for help, half-hearted, the echo of his lone voice losing itself in the trees.

THIS TRAILER IS FREE

Let's just say we never robbed the bank. Let's say we never sat there in the middle of that mobile home park outside of Dallas—our little trailer was the worst of the bunch—wondering how we got ourselves into this mess, no money for food or the light bill, even though it's no mystery to figure out. Jesse had just wrangled us a car to drive, one of them old-fashioned-looking PT Cruisers. The car was purple-pink with sparkles, a custom job, which was probably why Jesse's dad got it for him so cheap. His dad's name is Jody, which sounds like he'd be young and good-looking, like a movie star, but he's actually a real fat man and crippled up, too, from some accident. In fact, Jody's so bad off he can't even drive, so he'd had the car put on a hauler and another man drove him and the car down from Missouri. He wasn't exactly happy about it and he said the Cruiser would be the last thing he ever gave Jesse, this son that couldn't seem to keep a job or stay out of prison. From here on out, he was on his own.

So let's just pretend I didn't stare out at that purple car, thinking how it had a sheen like the oily puddles at the gas station, then straight at Jesse and say, "What we need is to come into a windfall. Money with no strings attached." Let's say I didn't see it right then, a running surge of electricity travel through that man, zip up along his spine and into his face so that his eyes, which he'd barely bothered to open before then, blinked alive and not with hope, but with a meanness I should've known was there all along. Let's say he had me fooled good and proper, even though I know all I was doing was turning my face the other way like I'd do with a wild dog, like if I avoided the eyes, that alone would keep it from lunging into me, snapping me at the neck and shaking me dead. Sometimes if you don't provoke it, meanness will leave you alone.

But it don't really work like that. You might not go looking for it, but meanness'll find you when it's ready. I can *what if* my way all the way back to the start with Jesse and it turns out the same: me, here, behind bars in a state that'd just as soon throw me in a pit or kill me stone cold than bother to ask me why we did it. I can go back to that shitty trailer, back to Idaho, back further to when I hurt my neck in the Army and got my taste for Oxy, back to when I had my baby, Jonathan, on my own, back even to when I got pregnant, and on and on and on, and it's like every move I made was the wrong one. But is it wrong if you can't seem to avoid it?

Me, I think I inherited my bad judgment, a family trait that won't let me go. When I was nine years old, me and my family was living in Arkansas, a little place called Greenwood, and I never knew why, but my dad came home one day with the frame of a hauler and a stack of plywood and with it he built this flimsy little trailer. He painted it lime green—he said the paint was on sale—and stenciled our family's last name on it in red, so that it looked like it was rigged out for Christmas. This was before him and my mom got divorced and she remarried, twice, to men who would've given anything if I'd just disappeared. My dad was prouder of that trailer than anything he'd ever done before, and I thought maybe we was going to use it to go on a vacation, something we'd never done before, but then he announced that we was packing up and heading to Alaska. "To do what?" my mom asked, and he said, "To work in the canning factories. Canning salmon."

My mom cried all night and said she would *not* go to Alaska, but my dad had quit his job already and convinced himself this was our one shot at happiness. "We'll make our money and be done," he said. "One season, maybe two, and we're out." We boxed up what would fit from the house we were renting into the lime-green hauler, and the rest we gave away or took to the dump. Me and my brothers sat in the wide backseat of the family car, the youngest of the two boys squeezed into the middle where he read his comic books the entire way, his legs crossed under him, Indian style. It was the longest drive I've ever been on and the whole time my dad was talking about Alaska being the last frontier, a place where a man like him could still make his fortune. We was on our last hundred miles and everyone in the car was asleep but my dad and me, and I looked out into the dark, the light from the moon shining down on the road so it was like we was driving on a sheet of silver. In the rearview mirror, my dad's eyes looked back at me and I saw the wrinkles at the edges turn up. He was happy and right there in that quiet Alaska night, I was happy, too.

It didn't last. Canning was brutal, way worse than working in the appliance factory back home, and my mom stopped smelling like my mom and started smelling like cooked fish and sweat and onions. She wouldn't even speak to my dad and we stopped eating supper at the table—one of the few good things we brought—in part because the two of them was too tired to sit up straight in a hard chair, but mainly because they couldn't stand the sight of one another. Me and my brothers took ourselves to school, where no one really talked to us, I think, because every kid there knew we wasn't going to stay. My mom told me years later that them Alaskans, the ones born and raised there, had watched people like us come and go for years, laughing at our ideas of getting rich quick packing fish or working the oil lines. We was fools to think we were tough enough for a country like theirs. They knew we'd never last.

None of us said one word as we packed up the trailer again and left Alaska. When my dad looked in the rearview mirror, it was just to see the road behind him, not to catch my eye. Truth was, I was glad it had all gone bust because I hated the cold I couldn't shake out of my hands and how my nose kept running so much that I had to slurp up snot with nearly every breath I took. It wasn't what you picture, Alaska, them swarms of mosquitoes and even quicksand, which swallowed up a woman who'd gotten a truck wheel lodged in it and got out to try to push the truck free, only to be sucked down herself. The kids at school said that when they pulled her body out of the sand, the suction took off one of her feet.

I missed Arkansas and I rested my head on the cold window and smiled to myself, thinking of warmer days ahead. That was when my head knocked against the glass and I heard my dad say, "Shit fire," and then the whole car was wobbling like we was driving over boulders. On the side of the road, me and my mom and dad and brothers got out, and we saw what was wrong, that not just one, but both of the tires had gone flat on the trailer, one split all along the outer ridge so it was nothing but a flap of black rubber. We had one spare, but not two and, of course, we didn't have no Triple A. It wasn't quite dark and the sky out on the horizon was purple and orange and if we hadn't been stranded out on some dead quiet road in Wyoming, I would've said it was pretty. Then my dad said what we all must've been thinking, that we'd have to leave the trailer behind.

He opened up the trailer and we took out what we could squeeze in around us in the car, and my mom actually got up in my dad's face and hissed at him and made like she was going to scratch out his eyes with her fingers, she was so mad. "My God, my table." Her voice cracked from the tears. "That was my mother's." But what else could we do? We were out there for more than an hour trying to get ourselves all situated and in that time, not a soul came by. We didn't see so much as a single light anywhere around and all you could hear was the sound of an owl somewhere up in a cluster of trees, hoot-hooting and then a kind of rattle and swoosh as it floated down out of the branches and right over our heads. On the hood of the car, my dad wrote on a piece of paper with a Magic Marker he'd took out of my school bag. He scribbled something down and rummaged through his toolbox and found a roll of black electrical tape and he ripped off two big, long strips and held the paper up against the plywood and taped it there on the doors. In all caps, he'd written THIS TRAILER IS FREE. "Let somebody else take it," he said to me. "I give up."

I could say that things went back to normal from there, that we settled down in Greenwood again and my dad went back to the appliance factory, but his job was long gone. I could say that my folks even learned to laugh about those three miserable months in Alaska and the trailer and all the things we left by the roadside in Wyoming, that they knew there was nothing in that trailer that we couldn't replace, but that would be a lie, too. Just like it'd be a lie to say I kept my head on straight in high school and then got myself a decent job and never was so dumb as to wander all the way off to a place like Idaho with a guy I'd met when I was in the Army—I was a terrible soldier, by the way, no point in pretending otherwise. When that guy was done, there was another, and another one after that and, all the while, I was wondering at what point I would give up and head back home, though I wasn't even sure where exactly that was by then.

I'd like to say that I had my baby boy and I took good care of him and it was all right that it was just him and me because, really, two people don't need that much and I was capable of raising a child, wasn't I? That I took up with Jesse because he was better than most and he had family with a big farm back in Missouri that sounded like a respectable way to make a living, but it was really that he liked painkillers as much as me and, if you didn't already know this, Oxy don't come cheap, which is why we thought we might get jobs in Texas, and we didn't even bother to get a trailer to haul our shit because all we had was a few clothes and some dishes and we put those in two cardboard boxes that we held on our laps on the Greyhound. I could say that I threw a fit the first time the social workers came and knocked on the door and asked if I knew that Jonathan was eating a candy bar for lunch every day and the principal of his school said he had a terrible smell and someone needed to wash his clothes. I could say that we robbed that bank because I needed the money for my kid and Jesse didn't want nobody to take him from us, either, and so we did it for love.

I might not have been looking for meanness, but it found me, and we didn't think to get in that ugly PT Cruiser—a stupid choice for a getaway car—and roll up in front of that bank and put a pair of cheap pantyhose over Jesse's face until a day or two after Jonathan was gone—maybe longer—when I'd woke up that morning with my heart racing in my chest, a weight on me like grief. What did I say when those women came to get him? I remember them there at the door, holding up some piece of paper with words too small to read, and I felt like I was about to come apart inside and I wanted to rip up what wasn't already in shreds in that trailer as my Jonathan walked down the cinder block steps, some other woman's hand on his shoulder. *Take him,* I know I said, and I doubt they were surprised. They'd seen my kind before and they knew I'd never last. Maybe Jonathan knew it, too. I keep saying it won't all come back to me, the rest of it, what I said and did that day, that something is blocked in my brain, but what's blocked my memory is me.

Let's say it was Jesse's fault for bringing us to Texas or Jonathan's dad for cutting out before my boy was born or the Army's for letting me get hurt or my mom and dad for fucking things up all those years ago in Arkansas, but I know it's not true. It isn't the women screaming for the guard up and down the corridor that wakes me in my cell but my own conscience that grabs me by the neck, looks me in the eye, making sure I know the meanness don't come from somewhere else, only from me. It's my own voice talking. I hear what I said. *Let somebody else have him. I give up.*

UNNATURAL HABITATS

Layton buzzes over his three-acre lot, the riding mower knocked into high gear. He loves this mower, which he bought mostly for its cool-looking roll bar. His wife told him to get one with a canopy. Sheila tells him to wear a hat, too, because his hair is thinning at the crest of his head, but hats are for pussies. So are canopies. The mower is black with yellow stripes—like a sweat bee—and was the most expensive model on the floor at Lowe's. He paid for it with his debit card, shielding his fingers from the customers in line behind him while he punched in the PIN. There are wolves all around and he can't be too careful. This is a fact he learned the hard way when his old business partner betrayed him. It was Gary, he was sure, who'd had him hunted down like an animal in the dark and beaten nearly to death. He hadn't gotten a good look at his attackers that night, and in his memory doesn't see blurs of men's faces or arms or the weapons they used to bring him down, but only the color of the pain, the blows replaying in his mind in bursts of red and purple and green.

But that was years ago and his life has changed since then. He lives now in a subdivision of garishly overbuilt houses, designed to evoke what the developer calls "a unique tradition of Southern glamour and grace." He thinks they look like the red brick fraternity house he lived in for two semesters, the houses' thick, white columns a nod to some antebellum fantasy. His neighbors are businessmen and bankers or big honchos at Tyson—Arkansas's new rich—and like him, bought there mostly for the size of the houses—a required minimum of six thousand square feet!—rather than the architecture.

But unlike him, none of his neighbors have any interest in mowing their own lawns. They hire the job out and, several times a week, a small army of brown-skinned laborers descends on the subdivision. They skim across the zoysia on stand-up mowers, whipping them under their boots like surfboards, filling the air with gas fumes. When the laborers finish mowing, they march over the hilly acres with trimmers and blowers, their mouths and noses hidden behind brightly colored bandanas. *Bandidos,* he calls them. If he wanted, he could hire his own crew of bandidos, but he considers his ride time on the sweat bee a necessary moment of solitude, when he can indulge in a fat joint without disruption, the smoke drifting up and over his head and beyond the boundaries of the subdivision.

Over the growl of the mower, he hears his children scream as they jump off the diving board into the pool. His oldest son, Elijah, appears to be drowning one of the younger kids. The water is roiling, two hands thrashing above the surface. Elijah's shaggy brown hair drips over his eyes so that all Layton can see of his face is a mean grin. He waves at him and shakes his head *no*. Elijah ducks into the water and the drowning child bursts up, gasping for breath, and punches him in the side of the head.

Layton drives on, steering the mower near his eastern neighbor's property. Though the green space between the houses is supposed to be left open, a few months earlier, the couple petitioned for special permission to install a wrought iron fence with spear-like points at the top, dividing their property from his. They're old, the man and woman, and spend their days on the golf course behind the houses, the electric green grass ending at a steep ravine. Layton doesn't play golf and doesn't't appreciate the balls that so often land in his yard. Elmo, his bichon frise, once managed to get one stuck in its mouth so that he had to wedge his fingers between its jaws to pry it out. Elmo is not a smart dog, the last of the pack Sheila used to breed when they lived on a small farm near the Missouri state line. Ahead of him lies another white ball and he speeds up and runs over it. The ball pings against one of the points of the speared fence.

This is when he sees them.

The old man stands there in his aqua-blue Bermudas, white socks pulled up over his ankles, his wife beside him. She's too thin, but Layton can tell she had been beautiful once. Probably even hot. What remains of her younger self hasn't left her the way it does most women, who seem to dissolve within themselves as they age, any beauty disappearing beneath rolls of belly fat and teased-up Brillo pads of hair. Her hair is cut in an elegant bob, the color of ice. He doesn't dislike the couple, but he's fairly sure they are not in love with him or his family. Still, they haven't been aggressive toward him. They haven't reported the extra storage shed he built, strictly forbidden under subdivision by-laws, or even the young deer he captured and kept as a pet for the kids until it died for no reason at all. Nearing them, he smiles and offers a kind of salute, but they don't respond. Maybe they don't see him?

Closer, he waves again, but it's as if the couple is posing for a picture. The woman's flamingo pink sarong flutters against her legs. He puts the mower in park, slides his sunglasses onto the top of his head, and squints his eyes, the joint clamped tightly between his front teeth. He takes one long, last draw and holds the smoke in his lungs an extra count of three before he exhales, tossing the stub on the lawn. Near the neighbors' pool, he sees it, the cat laid out beneath a chaise lounge, thick forearms stretched in front of her. The bob of her tail twitches.

"Hey," he says, but the old couple's eyes are fixed on the bobcat, a stare they don't break even while he opens the gate and slowly steps toward the patio. "You want me to get her?"

They remain frozen. *Fuck. She's not a goddamn cheetah.* He would've said this out loud when he was younger, but he's learned you can keep some thoughts to yourself—a lesson that has improved his business, which has, in turn, made the house and the pool and the fancy subdivision possible. His wife is thrilled to be a resident of The Estates at Devil's Den, a name he would've thought laughable had it not been for the word "devil." That part he secretly thinks appropriate.

"It's really all right to move. She isn't a grizzly bear, you know. Just a bobcat. Bobbie's a pet."

"Still wild." The old man speaks, trying not to move his lips so that he looks and sounds like a bad ventriloquist.

"Listen," says Layton. "I've got children. What kind of dad would keep a wild animal around his own kids?" Bobbie is supposed to stay in her pen at all times. If the kids want to play with her, they have to go inside the pen, too, and close the latch behind them. To keep a bobcat as a pet, he is supposed to have a permit with the county, but he never bothered with it. She belonged first to Gary and all her original paperwork is still in his name. Layton did not want to explain how he'd come to have the cat himself. Besides, he thinks the paperwork for animals and houses and cars is almost certainly a violation of his rights as an American citizen, and as long as nobody gets all pissy about the cat and calls the sheriff, why does it matter?

He bends down and looks under the chaise lounge, snaps his fingers at the cat. She blinks, sleepy in the heat, and turns her face away. He slips two fingers beneath her orange mesh collar and gives a tug. She's old for a bobcat but strong, and she somehow makes her body heavier than it is and growls, a warning rumbling from her chest.

"You. Better. Be. Careful." The old man is still being a ventriloquist. The cat's body tightens as Layton drags her to him, her claws scraping against the bricks.

"Fine, motherfucker," he whispers. "Make it hard for me." He takes the beach towel draped over the lounger and scoots closer to the cat. "Here." He offers his hand for her to sniff.

She refuses to budge. He picks Bobbie up off the ground by the collar and she begins to fight him, claws pushing out of the pads of her toes. He swaddles her in the towel and presses her to his chest. He checks out his frozen neighbors. The man glares at him, eyes watery from not blinking for so long. He will definitely call the sheriff.

The cat growls again and Layton feels her body tighten, like she is winding herself up to let loose a tornado of fur and spit. A stream of warm piss spreads through the towel and saturates his t-shirt.

"Okay, we're going now." He tries to say it as if nothing has happened, the way he might talk to a small child. "Call if you need anything." His friendly tone won't do any good. Arms tiring from clutching the cat, he walks as fast as he can to his own backyard, breathing through his mouth to avoid the rising smell of ammonia. The cat's pen is behind the pool, the front latch open. Inside the pen, he squats down and throws the cat to the corner before he escapes out the gate, locking it behind him.

He pulls off his shirt. The back is still dry and he brushes it over his stomach to rub off the urine. It's nearly impossible to get the smell of bobcat piss out of clothes—another thing he has learned the hard way—and he wads up the shirt and hurls it toward the pool. He does the same thing to the towel, which lands just shy of the water near the edge where his daughter rests her head on her arms while she practices kicking her legs out behind her. Her head bolts up when the towel lands in front of her face and she lets out a screech of surprise. Then she gags, making a choking sound, and pinches at her nose before she lunges backward and disappears beneath the water.

"Guess what I found in the mailbox today?" Sheila says. Her hair is different than it was this morning when Layton left for Insure-U. Her nails are newly painted, too, with tiny rhinestones lined along the tips. When they first met, she had brown hair bleached through in thick chunks of white so that she looked like she could be in a band. They spent a lot of nights at River City, a club down on College Avenue that had nasty green turf for carpeting and was frequented by sorority and fraternity kids and a shocking number of drug dealers. Sheila partied back then, but she wouldn't do the things he demanded of other girlfriends, like giving hand-jobs to his coked-up friends or ferrying bags of weed around in the glove compartment of her car. She told him straight out that she wasn't some whore. Strangely, it was her defiance that attracted him and they've been together ever since, even though he's run around on her plenty. If Sheila knows, she doesn't let on.

"Just tell me," he says. "I hate guessing."

"A letter from Animal Control." She picks the envelope off the counter and waves it in front of his face.

"Why?" He grabs her wrist and takes it from her hand. Though she's put on weight the last couple of years, her wrists are still thin and bony.

"Why do you think? It's about Bobbie, of course."

It's been two weeks since Bobbie's visit to the neighbors'. He figured the old man and woman decided complaining wasn't worth the energy. He reads the letter, crumples it, and throws it into the corner of the room. Paper towels dot the carpet, a pile of guinea pig turds hidden beneath each one. He won't pay for a lawn service, but he's fine with housekeepers. It's expensive, though, and he's committed to getting the most for his money, so no one in the family is to so much as pick up a pair of dirty underwear before each week's cleaning. The guinea pig belongs to his daughter, their only girl, and is allowed to run free through the house, which also means it's allowed to shit wherever it wants. It was his idea to simply cover the crap piles with paper towels, leaving them for the housekeepers to deal with.

"You better take it serious, Layton." Sheila looks at her cell phone and frowns. "We'll get fined. I've got enough problems with Elijah."

"So?"

Her fingers flick over the phone screen. Sheila is never without her phone. "He's our son and he's turning into a little monster. Don't you listen?"

"I mean about getting fined. I've got the money, so what's the problem?"

She puts her phone on the counter, covering it with her hand. "Do I really have to explain this to you? We don't live out in the country, Layton. We signed a contract when we moved in. There are rules here." She releases a loud breath of exasperation. "I don't like that damn cat anyway. You've been pushing your luck all along. You should get rid of it."

"What do you care about the cat?"

She picks up her phone again. "It's where it came from, what all was going on then. I don't like the memory."

"Not that shit again." He throws his hands up, then points a finger at her, holding it just inches from her nose. "Just shut your face, Sheila." He gives her the hardest look he can. At the church she makes them go to, the preacher likes to go on about how a husband should respect his wife, how he should treat her like a gift from God. Layton can't take the man seriously, not with the gelled hair and the pitiful soul patch beneath his bottom lip. Layton is who he is, a man not so different from the one he had been seven years ago. Fatter now, sure, and he wears khakis every day, but he is still the guy who stole Bobbie and those big, dumb dogs. He is still the guy who beat the fuck out of Gary, who got his revenge. He can still do whatever he wants.

Gary. Layton wakes in the middle of the night, his mind too alive with thoughts of his old business partner to go back to sleep. Where is Gary now? Layton used to think about him all the time. They had a good thing going—Layton running the office, Gary doing the adjustments and handling the drugs—right up until the day Layton was nearly killed. It happened outside an apartment complex a block from the university, where he went to meet some college kids who wanted to buy a little Ecstasy. There was a woman he was seeing and he intended to meet up with her when he was done. It should've been a simple drop, but something went wrong. His car door was yanked open and he felt hands pulling him out before he fell to the asphalt. Men had him—he didn't know how many—and they were hitting him, but why? And with what? Fists couldn't be that hard. Covering his head with his arms, he looked up just once to catch a glimpse of what was coming down on him. Baseball bats. He didn't remember what happened between the final slam to the back of his skull and waking up days later in a hospital bed. When he opened his eyes, he saw his father's fat head above him, lips murmuring in prayer.

It took months before he was back on his feet and, in the meantime, Gary was in charge at Insure-U. Layton was bad off, his mind foggy from painkillers, but even in that state he saw how much Gary enjoyed running the business on his own. That was the first clue that he was behind the attack. It was all about power, about envy. Gary was jealous of Layton, but it made sense. It was Layton who had the rich father, who managed to finish college, graduating with a degree in business despite being stoned nearly every day for his last three semesters.

A part of him, though, wanted to give Gary a chance to come clean, to repent. "Tell me who you think did this to me," he said to him. He was home from the hospital then, but could barely walk on his own and it was painful to sit up straight and talk. Three of his ribs were cracked all the way through and the doctor said he'd been fortunate to not have a punctured lung.

Gary didn't even flinch at the question. "You don't know?"

"No, I don't know. Tell me."

"Your girlfriend's husband, of course."

Anger boiled up in him, settling in his throat. "Husband? They're separated. He's not even around."

"And that means exactly shit. You were plowing another man's field and you got found out. Think about what you'd do if you found out Sheila was fucking somebody else."

"So you think it was cool for somebody to do this to me?"

"Not cool at all." Gary sat with his legs crossed and unwrapped a piece of hard caramel someone had put beside Layton's bed and popped it into his mouth. "Just logical. I think the bastard should've taken it out on his woman, not you, but that's not how it went. Obviously."

That was when he made up his mind. Gary was too quick to blame someone else. Retaliation was non-negotiable. The trap at the old battlefield, the beating was completely justifiable. But why was it bothering him after all this time? Gary was a moron to fuck with him, yet, with each passing year—Layton will turn forty in November—he feels a stinging wave of sadness about it, a feeling that pinches inside his stomach. Worse still is a haunting, new doubt that he can't seem to shake.

If Gary really was the one who hurt him, that meant his instincts about him had been wrong from the start, and if a man can't rely on his instincts, what chance does he have to protect himself? When he met Gary, he'd instantly trusted him in a way he had no one else and confided in him as he might have a brother. At Insure-U, Gary had few qualms about dealing with the Dallas assholes, meeting up with them in middle-of-nowhere Oklahoma and Arkansas and Texas to make trades of drugs and money. He never got hassled by the state patrols and, even if he had, he'd have known what to do. Gary even liked the legitimate part of Insure-U and was good at checking out wrecks and assessing claims. He knew a lot about cars—he'd worked on them with his dad out at the house where he later lived with the girl from the office with the bleached-out hair, with his dogs and birds and snakes and the bobcat. Layton likes to imagine that Gary and the animals are still there and the thought brings him comfort, which bothers him even more.

He can't fall back to sleep, so he goes downstairs and plops into the big recliner, a giant, brown marshmallow, and sinks deep into its cushions. The electric hum of the cicadas outside rises and falls. Holes pockmark the ground where the insects have crawled out of their seven- and fourteen-year beds to take their place up and down the bark of the trees, red-eyed aliens splitting from their husks. They're so loud this year that some people wear earplugs to keep from getting headaches. It sounds like the cicadas are right there in the room with him, and he looks to the sliding glass door—which is open. He shut and locked the door himself before going to bed, but someone's come in or gone out since then.

Sheila thinks Elijah has been sneaking out at night, then coming back and making a mess. She finds wrappers from Ho-Ho's and Ding-Dongs and Pop-Tarts scattered over the kitchen counters and floor. When she finally confronted Elijah, he merely raised a single eyebrow and looked pointedly at the muffin top spilling over her jeans: maybe she had eaten all the snacks herself? "He's completely disrespectful, Layton. It's like he doesn't even recognize authority anymore. He used to be the sweetest kid, but now he just acts like he hates everybody."

Layton shrugged away any concern. Elijah has always been an unremarkable child, easy to ignore. He remembers little from the time when Elijah was born—only that his birth changed Sheila. She was so adoring of Layton during the pregnancy—pathetically so—while he occupied himself with Insure-U, barely acknowledging their coming child. His father bought the franchise for him and he felt weighing on him the pressure of the man's expectations. He suspected he was a disappointment to his father, and that became his excuse for creating the illegal side of the business. The drugs guaranteed a positive inflow of cash but were also an act of quiet rebellion, a secret he held back, like a weapon. Another child followed Elijah two years later, then another and another, but Layton has little connection to any of them.

Elijah's never seemed to care that Layton and he aren't close. Once, when the boy was probably no older than eight, Layton watched him skid out on his bike, his face plowing into the pink gravel road in front of their old house. He rushed to his son, who sat stunned in the middle of the road before he wiped his hand across his lips, smearing blood over his cheeks. Layton tried to take him into his arms, but Elijah's body went stiff at his touch. Sheila came running from the house and Elijah let her clean his face with a dampened washcloth. Between them was a tenderness

Layton hadn't noticed before and he'd been struck by the unfamiliar feelings of love and jealousy.

He starts to turn on the patio light but stops himself. If it is Elijah out here, he wants to surprise him, to catch him in the act, whatever that might be. He hesitates but decides to leave behind the baseball bat he keeps by the door.

There is no one on the patio. He steps into the yard. The dark makes him feel off-balance and he walks with his hands out to his sides. He listens for a hint of someone in the darkness, but it's hard to hear anything over the cicadas. A ripple of fear hisses up his spine and he thinks he senses the presence of someone near. His ribs begin to ache, a phantom reaction he's had dozens of times since the beating. "Hey, who's there?" he says.

He hears a cough and then the sound of laughter, too high-pitched to be Elijah's. Until now, it hasn't occurred to him that Elijah might be running around with a girl. That's all he needs. God, he doesn't want to take care of some teenager's baby. "Is that you, Eli?" he calls. "You better get your skinny ass in the house."

He waits for his son to rush out of the darkness and into the dim light, but nothing happens. He calms himself and swallows, disgusted with his own fear. Elijah is just a teenager—his own teenager. The cicadas seem to hum louder. He returns to the house, sliding the door closed behind him. He sinks into the recliner, reaches over to the lamp and pulls the chain and the room goes dark. He'll just sleep here. If he returns to his room Sheila will wake up and ask him a million questions. The conversation will drag on all night. He crosses his arms over his chest and takes a deep breath and feels himself getting groggy, his body relaxing into the big brown marshmallow. The noise of the cicadas fades away and he dreams that he hears footsteps coming nearer, nearer, then a man standing over him.

"Hey, Dad," says the voice. He opens his eyes, smelling beef jerky and beer, maybe peanut butter. Elijah's face is above him, upside down as the boy looks at him from behind the chair. With his hair hanging down around his face, he looks like a wolf. "What are you doing down here?" Elijah presses down on the back of the recliner, rocking it up and down as if he means to catapult him into the air, before he releases it and climbs the stairs to his room.

"It was Elijah," Layton tells Sheila the next morning. He's dressed in khakis and his blue oxford button-down. A couple of years ago, he had the Insure-U emblem embroidered on the chest pockets of his shirts and bought matching ones for the agents and secretaries to wear, too. After a while, though, it made him feel stupid, like he was working at a grocery store or Walmart, and he made everyone stop. Gary would've hated the matching clothes, he thought as he collected the shirts and threw them in the trash.

"It was Elijah what?"

"Who's been sneaking down here. He's probably the one who let Bobbie out, too. He was with a girl."

"Did she have red hair?"

"I don't know. I couldn't see anything in the dark. I just heard somebody laughing."

"Well, you told him that he's done with it, right? That he's grounded for the rest of the summer?"

He turns his back and digs down in a kitchen drawer to find his keys. "He went to bed. I fell sleep."

"Goddamn it, Layton." She punches him between his shoulder blades. "Could you help me with a little discipline here?"

"He knows I know, so he'll lay off," he says. "And don't hit me. You know I don't like that."

She puts her fists on her hipbones and stares at him. He hates it when she acts as if she has the right to threaten him. She needs to be grateful for what she has, the big house, the pool, the money, the cars. "By the way," she says. Her voice is spiteful. "I saw Animal Control cruising by first thing this morning. You better make sure your cat's where it's supposed to be."

"She is. And the lock's got a combination on it, so they'll have to break in to get her."

"God. You act like that animal's something valuable, like it's something that matters to you. I don't get it."

"She is valuable," he says. "She's mine. I took her and she's mine. Animal Control can fuck off."

"You took her so she's yours so she's valuable. That makes no sense, Layton. And what's with this 'she' business? Bobbie's an 'it.' Animals are 'its,' Layton."

He doesn't bother to answer. Who does she think she is? An English teacher? This is life with her now, going round and round about everything. For years, she was complacent, rarely questioning him. But something changed during her pregnancy with their fourth and last child, when she told him she didn't feel right living a life paid for by illegal activities. She said she'd had a spiritual awakening, complete with a new vision for her family. She started taking the kids to church, a non-denominational congregation in Bella Vista, and recommitted her life to Christ.

By then, Layton's father had figured out the truth behind Insure-U's swollen profits, expressing his disapproval through the worst way possible: silence. For a hardcore Presbyterian, his father had an odd take on God and retribution. He didn't believe that God punished those who went astray or withheld blessings, but merely removed himself from the presence of the guilty, leaving them to survive in the isolation of their own poor judgment, and as a parent, his response to bad behavior was the same. Between the pressures of his wife and father, there seemed to Layton little point in resisting reform. He was tired and, without Gary, had no one to do the dirtiest work. The guy who helped with Gary's beating—a failed car salesman, which should've been a clue that he would suck at insurance and dealing—turned out to be an idiot who quickly lost interest in the practicalities of the business. Layton was alone at Insure-U and he had nothing to lose by getting his shit together. And, like his father's business, the insurance firm turned out to be a success once he focused on it. The world churned up a mountain of high-risk clients every day, their premiums far exceeding what the company paid out in settlements. The drug suppliers simply fell away from inattention, showing him how powerful neglect could be.

"Listen," he says. "I'll go to the county office and talk to Animal Control, okay? I'll see about getting the license for Bobbie, then everybody will be happy."

"Happy? Whatever."

Getting the license for Bobbie requires that he prove the cat is up-to-date on her shots and that a county inspector certify the cage she stays in is both large enough to be considered humane and secure enough to ensure she can never escape. There is no way he'll let an inspector on his property, some government asshole on a power trip who could nose his way into anything he wanted, dinging Layton for any number of violations. Problem is, now that he's tipped his hand that he has a non-domesticated animal in his possession, the county says he has only three weeks to comply. "What if I don't want to?" he asks the desk clerk.

"The animal will be taken away and destroyed."

"Destroyed?"

"Put down."

"Killed?" he says. The clerk gives him a blank look, blinking her eyes in a way that reminds him of Bobbie.

"That's exactly what that means." She speaks in a tone she must reserve for the elderly and morons. But he's just trying to get things straight before he gets pushed into anything.

"Are we done?" the clerk says. Before he can even step aside, she clicks the remote to the digital sign above her head and calls out the next number. He wants to tell the rude woman he's a tax-paying citizen. He drives a Cadillac Escalade. The SUV cost $75,000 and he has so much insurance on it, he could crash it straight into the building and never pay a dime.

He does learn something useful at the county office, though. There are no past records on Bobbie after all. Gary never had a license to keep her, though Layton is sure that he remembers him saying she had shots for rabies and distemper. Gary might have done those himself, gotten the vaccinations from a vet that came out to the surrounding farms to check cattle and horses. Gary's place was so far out in the country, he could've kept the cat a secret. He let Bobbie roam freely, coming in and going out of the house through a flap installed in the back door. Even now, Layton thinks it was one of the coolest things he's ever seen, Bobbie climbing down out of a tree with a squirrel or an entire bird's nest in her mouth, then lumbering across the yard and into the house to flop down in front of the TV and sleep. She ignored her prey, left to linger in pain until Gary took the creature outside and finished it off.

The morning he smuggled the cat from Gary's, he was high from snorting two long lines of cocaine and, as a result, his memory was fuzzy, though he could still picture the image of the guy who came along to help—the prospective new partner—and how Bobbie quickly slashed him across the lips, the blood dripping down his mouth so the guy looked like a vampire. Later, the two of them used a crowbar and a tire iron to beat Gary, chopping down on him like they were splitting wood, blood seeping from the wounds so fast that, at first, Layton thought it was piss that darkened Gary's jeans. Then he saw the broken leg bone, jagged and poking through the skin, Gary's body cracking apart from the inside out. He smelled the rank odor of shit, and collapsed onto his knees, turned his head to the side, and choked. He was overcome by the savage intimacy of it—the unmaking of another man's body—and a sting of stomach acid surged into his throat. He was euphoric, pumped full of adrenaline, until he saw what he'd done to Gary, and was dizzy and sick, his own body beginning to shake. All he could think to do was get in his car and drive away.

"The neighbors won't speak to me," Sheila says. "Thanks a lot, Layton." He has just come in the door from the garage and hasn't even set down his keys.

She's ordered pizza for supper and divides it onto paper plates for the kids. They're all at the table, even Elijah, who rarely joins the family for meals. Layton has no idea what he does instead. The house is so large, it's easy to lose a child in the maze of rooms, but in the last few days, Elijah has been more present than he's been in weeks. In fact, since having his keys taken away—Sheila also put a lock on the steering wheel of his car—he's made himself impossible to miss, camping out in the living room in front of the big screen TV and refusing to let anyone else have the remote. It doesn't matter. They have four other TVs and the other children merely drift off to various rooms by themselves. Elijah is sprawled on the marshmallow recliner in the morning when Layton walks through the living room to the kitchen to get his coffee, and the kid is still there when he arrives home at the end of the day. Does he get up for anything? To eat? To go to the bathroom? Sheila says he does, but when Layton's home, Elijah never so much as turns his head to acknowledge a visitor to the room. The other kids don't bother to enter the living room anymore, their brother's mere presence having become a threat.

"Did you hear what I said? I'm sick of this whole thing with Bobbie," Sheila says.

"I don't want to listen to this tonight. Drop it."

"Did you go to Animal Control?"

"Yes, last week. Again, drop it."

"And?"

His mouth is full of pizza. Only one of the children likes pineapple, so Sheila orders one side of his pizza with it. His side is meat lover's, but a pineapple tidbit has made its way over onto the pepperoni, sausage, and hamburger. The pineapple squishes between his molars and he spits it out.

"And there's all this shit I have to do to keep the fucking cat." He's not supposed to use bad language in front of the kids. Sheila worries they will repeat it at school or at church.

"Are you going to? Because it won't make things better. I can tell." Sheila doesn't bother to correct his language. "These people here think we're a bunch of hillbillies, Layton."

"Right," he says, flatly. If he refuses to show emotion, maybe she'll shut up.

"We aren't hillbillies, are we?" their daughter asks. She's a pretty girl with blue eyes and delicate, pale skin, ginger freckles scattered over her nose, and looks wholesome enough to be on the Disney Channel. Recently, she's grown sensitive to words like "hillbilly" and "redneck." It started after they took the kids to Silver Dollar City earlier in the summer. She watched intently the basketmakers and blacksmiths in their old-timey clothes, the women in bonnets, the men with long, white beards. Later, when the family ate at a giant buffet restaurant, the streets of Branson glittering like a small-time Vegas outside the window of their booth, an excessively fat family pushed their way to the front of the line and filled their plates until they were heaped with pyramids of food covered in salad dressing and gravy. Behind them a man pretended to whisper. "Those are the real fuckin' hillbillies," he said, looking around to make sure someone was listening. "Inbred hogs."

"No, baby, we're not hillbillies," Sheila says. "We're just from Arkansas. We're normal."

He snorts. He doesn't mean to, but it's such a dishonest thing to say. The last thing they'd ever be is normal. He starts to laugh, and the swig of Coke he just swallowed works its way up into his nose and out onto his plate. The younger kids look at him and then at Sheila. They start to laugh, too. Sheila glares at him and takes a bite of pizza. Only she and Elijah do not find the whole thing hilarious. God, but the boy is becoming as humorless as his mother.

"I think you should release Bobbie back into the wild," Elijah says. The other kids' laughter has simmered down to random giggles and none of them are listening to their oldest brother. But Sheila and Layton look at each other. They haven't heard Elijah speak in days and this feels like a miracle.

"I agree." Sheila sits up straighter in her chair, empowered by Elijah's words.

"She shouldn't be caged up like she is," he says. "It isn't cool to do that to animals that are meant to be out in nature. It's just dickheads who try to turn them into pets."

"Elijah said the D word," his daughter says. "That means 'penis.'"

"Let me tell you something about this animal." Layton points his fork first at Sheila, then at Elijah. "This cat hasn't lived out in nature since she was a kitten and she won't know jack shit about how to get along without someone serving up a can of 9 Lives for her every day." He is lifting the rule about no cursing. It's his goddamn house and he can say what he goddamn wants.

"She doesn't eat 9 Lives," says Elijah. "She eats hamburger. Raw. Like a regular, wild animal."

"Wild animals eat other wild animals, not hamburger. And that's not the point." He isn't going to be told what to do by a pimple-faced teenager. "Trust me on this. She'll find her way straight to somebody else's back door and they won't be like 'Oh, sweet kitty cat.' They'll be like, 'Oh, shit, where's my gun?'"

"Not if you take her back where she came from. If she knows the territory, she'll stay where she belongs. Where'd you get her, anyway?"

"From a friend." He won't look at Sheila. She is glaring at him again.

"Then take her back to the friend."

"He's gone."

"To where?"

"Nobody knows. Into the fucking ether. But here's how it is: she's not going anywhere. I'll fix the cage. I'll deal with the inspector."

"But not the neighbors," Sheila says. "Because that's my job, right? Because you really don't give a shit if people look the other way when they see us coming. If everybody's scared to death of us. If they treat us like a bunch of outlaws."

The kids all get up and leave upon hearing their mother curse, except for Elijah, who clenches his fists, flexing his fingers out and in, nostrils flaring. When he was first born, Elijah had been the spitting image of him, but he'd changed soon after, morphing between a resemblance to Sheila and then to Layton's father. If the kid would cut his hair and trim the silly little excuse for a mustache above his lip, he'd be handsome. Instead, his hair grows wild, full with curls that twist into knots when he neglects to use a comb. Layton thinks of John the Baptist, running around in the wilderness, twigs and shit in his hair, probably smelling like a beast.

"You take her back." Elijah pushes his chair away from the table and stands. "Or I will. One way or another, Bobbie's going home."

The boy's hands are planted flat on the table, as though he's preparing to lunge across it. Skinny as he is, he's far from a threat, yet Layton braces himself. The boy's face has slimmed, his brow widened. His arms have grown wiry with new muscle that flexes at his wrists and forearms. Elijah's eyes twitch from staring so hard. This is a test, Layton understands, one that will determine who is in charge.

He stands up and crosses his arms over his chest. "I don't think you're in any position to be telling me what to do." He's putting an end to this right now. "And I'll be damned if I'm going to be bullied into doing anything by my own goddamn son. Bobbie is staying right here. This is my fucking castle, Elijah. This is my fucking kingdom."

The idea is to take Bobbie back to Gary's house, though Gary himself is no longer there. While Gary was in the hospital after the beating, the police questioned Layton about what might have happened to his business partner. Did Gary have any enemies? Had there been trouble, perhaps, with a customer angry over an adjustment? Had there been a conflict between them? When Layton asked who'd rescued Gary, they said a park ranger at the battlefield found him on her way home. He managed to push most of the suspicion onto the blonde girl from the office who also lived with Gary, who'd witnessed the beating before she ran off, literally, into the woods. He could never remember her name.

It was the blonde's own mother who helped him trap Gary. He'd given the silly woman one of Sheila's extra dogs and, after that, she started hanging around the office, wearing low-cut blouses and bending over every chance she got to show off her sagging tits. Her chest skin was like brown crepe paper from overtanning, and she was simultaneously sexy and repulsive. Her need for attention had made it easy to convince her to lure Gary onto one of the country roads up near Pea Ridge Battlefield, by calling him to say her car was dead. Gary arrived within the hour and, once he crawled under the car—Gary never hesitated to crawl under a car: Layton had watched him do it dozens of times—Layton and the other guy came out from the bushes, weapons already raised above their heads. It worked the way he'd planned and he was pleased that he knew Gary so well, that there was no way Gary could resist the chance to play hero. What he failed to plan for was the aftermath.

Being questioned scared the shit out of him. Why hadn't he considered that he would be the most obvious suspect? That someone would find Gary, that he wouldn't just disappear? Over the years, his father had taken care of most of his fuck-ups, but this was a new level of fuck-up, of the variety even the most powerful father might not be able to undo. Once the police dropped the case, the realization of how near he'd come to being caught—to being punished— settled on him like a dark epiphany. It gnawed at his mind and he knew he needed to make peace with Gary. He drove out to his place past Gravette and knocked on the door, but no one answered. Of course, the big dogs were gone—he'd taken them himself and dumped them over the Oklahoma border a couple weeks after he stole Bobbie—but when he pressed his face up against the living room window, he saw that all the terrariums and aquariums, once filled with snakes and fish and lizards, were gone, too. He went to the back of the house where Gary kept his birds. Even the big cockatiel was missing. The house was devoid of any life at all, animal or human.

Fayetteville was a small place and after asking around, he learned that though Gary survived, he wasn't well enough to live on his own and after the hospital, moved in with a cousin in Malvern while he went through physical therapy. Layton figured Gary would return to his own home someday and then there'd be a reckoning to be had, but wherever Gary had gone and whatever he'd done next, it hadn't included facing down Layton Vines.

"She doesn't want to go in the crate," says Elijah. It's Saturday morning, a time when Layton would prefer to sleep in, but, instead, here he is cornering Bobbie in her pen. The boy throws a towel over her, then quickly wraps her in it like a burrito, but two paws have already escaped the binding. Bobbie catches the sides of the crate opening and pushes against it. "She's crazy strong," Elijah says, panting.

"I wish I'd got some tranquilizers," Layton says. Any second now, Elijah is going to get clawed across the face, then he'll see how stupid this whole thing is, how unnecessary.

"Then she'd just be disoriented." Elijah squeezes his arms tighter around the cat. "You could've fed her some weed, I guess." Elijah's eyes squint at him. Does Elijah hate him? Can a son hate his father? As much as he rebelled against his own, he never hated him. He loved his father and, by every indication, his father loved him, too. All that was in between was a mystery, one that he hasn't worked hard enough to understand.

"I don't have any weed." He tries to stand taller, the way his father used to do when he had enough of Layton's smart mouth. Sheila says it's a father's duty to discipline his children and raise them up in the nurture and admonition of the Lord. He doesn't want to be that kind of father, maybe because he really doesn't care. He's consented to fatherhood but not to enjoying it. His tolerance seemed a compromise both he and Sheila, until recently, could equally accept.

"Fucker," Elijah says. Was he calling Layton a fucker? He was probably talking to the cat. "Maybe we could just leave her loose in the backseat?"

"Give her to me." Layton takes Bobbie, squeezing her close to his chest. Elijah stands beside him and he realizes that though the boy has grown tall, he'll probably never be as big as him. When Layton was a skinny teenager himself, he was broader across the chest and shoulders than Elijah.

Bobbie calms against him. Her back feet are enveloped within the towel and he slides her into the crate, back legs first, then snaps the door shut. The cat flips so violently that the crate tips over sideways, and she lets out a strange, high-pitched sound. Elijah straightens the crate in the backseat, but it flips again.

"Stop. She's pissed enough as it is. She doesn't want you to make it better." He pats the top of the crate before he closes the truck door. "Just leave her alone."

On the drive to Gravette, Elijah sits hunch-shouldered in the passenger seat, gnawing on a footlong stick of beef jerky.

"Where'd you get that?" They're passing by Fayetteville, the traffic already heavier from the students returning to the university.

"Mom gave it to me. I was hungry."

"Why don't you just wave it under Bobbie's nose, huh? Rile her up a little more?"

Elijah looks at the cat behind him and takes another bite off the stick before he pokes the rest into her crate.

"You didn't just give that to her, did you?"

"You made me feel bad about it. I couldn't just throw it out the window. That's littering."

Layton hadn't meant for him to throw it away, but the idea of a cord of beef jerky flying from the Escalade and thumping into the windshield of an unsuspecting driver strikes him as funny. His shoulders shake with the beginnings of laughter. Elijah curls his lips up in a snarl.

"What?" says Layton. "It's funny."

"I wasn't trying to be funny."

"Well, don't look like that, okay?"

"Like what?"

Layton makes the face, pulling his top lip up and panting.

"I don't look like that."

Layton glances down at the speedometer. He's going a good twenty miles over the limit, and taps the brake. The smell of urine wafts to the front seat. He hopes the piss doesn't slosh out of the crate onto the white leather seats.

"How far is this place?"

"A ways," Layton says. "What? You don't like the drive?"

Elijah stares ahead.

"Did you have plans or something?" He's not going to let Elijah give him the silent treatment. If the kid is mad about giving up his day to return the cat, he'll have to get over it. There are consequences for his actions. "You have a girl-friend, right? Some redhead?"

"She dyes it." He looks out the passenger window.

"She must be wild then."

"Don't make fun of her."

"I'm trying to figure out what she's like," says Layton. "Are you in love?"

Elijah leans his head against the back of the seat and closes his eyes. He crosses his arms over his stomach and takes a long, deep breath.

"I remember love," says Layton. "You gotta be careful with that. Don't do something stupid."

Elijah lets a puff of air out his nose and rolls his eyes. "You remember love? I bet."

The road has changed over the seven years since Layton was last at Gary's. The gravel is paved over and there's a new sign-post marking the road, a fence of painted black metal stretching on for a half mile. Everything out here is for sale now. Everything, that is, but Gary's place. It's simply been abandoned. The name "G. Moore" on the mailbox is barely visible beneath a layer of dust. There's no real driveway left and he worries about pulling in and accidentally dropping into a ditch.

The high wheels of the Escalade crush through the tall weeds. He's guessed right about where the drive is. The path leads into a field and ends at the bottom of a low hill. The house, still standing, doesn't look as bad as he figured it might. "Be careful when you get out. I bet it's real snakey around here."

"I don't mind snakes," Elijah says.

"You'd mind if you got bit by a copperhead. I knew a guy, growing up, who got bit out on some Boy Scouts campout."

"Did he die?"

"No." It would've made a better story if the kid died. "But he got plenty sick. They couldn't get him out before the swelling started, so someone had to hike back to get help. The rest who stayed with the guy said they thought his skin would burst open, his leg swelled up so big."

Elijah probably thinks he's lying, but he knows lots of snake stories and they're all true. In Ft. Smith, where he grew up, the Arkansas River flooded every few springs and the streets filled with enough water that his father took out the canoe and the two of them toured the neighborhoods. Once he saw a family of snakes, an adult and a dozen babies, like fat worms, gliding over the surface of the brown water. The snakes came right up next to the side of the canoe and he panicked, but his father didn't. His father pulled the paddle from the water and rested it on his knees, allowing the snake family to go by undisturbed. Layton had been told at school that reptiles didn't stay with their young, but his father said that wasn't true. "Not all the time," he said, digging his paddle into the water again. "One time I saw a nest of babies curled up in the tail of a big black snake, thick as my arm. It might've been waiting to eat those little ones, but it didn't look like it to me. We don't know everything about creation."

Layton wishes he'd worn his cowboy boots. The weeds are surely covered in chiggers and ticks. He'll be eaten up and Elijah, wearing thin, nylon shorts and Nike flip-flops will be, too. The kid waves his hands over the tips of the grass as if wading into the ocean. A spouting of grasshoppers flies up around him, one landing in his mess of hair, but he doesn't brush it away.

"Who lived here?"

"A friend."

They reach the house and Elijah peers through the front window. He walks around the side, out of view.

Layton opens the back door of the Escalade and puts on the leather gloves he brought. He pulls at the crate but smells the piss and doesn't want it spilling out if the whole thing tips over. When Bobbie is mad, she can make crazy things happen. Her anger gives her superpowers.

"Eli, come help me with this." He bends down to see the cat behind the wire door, her tongue hanging out of her mouth. She'll find something to drink once they let her out. There's a big pond on the acres behind the house. The water will be filthy, but she'll be all right.

A wind picks up and blows across the lawn, the weeds twisting and waving in all directions. He feels a prickle on his wrist that he's afraid is a spider, but it's only beggar's lice. The little burrs are stuck on his jeans and he starts plucking them off, but there are too many.

"Elijah," he calls again. "Come on." He wants to get going. He doesn't want to get close to the house, which is childish, but here it is again, a flashback of multicolored fireworks erupting in his thoughts. Gary is gone, the blonde is gone. There's nothing to fear, yet he feels his heart beating in his chest, a new pain stretching along his shoulders and into his arms.

Where is Elijah? He walks slowly down by the side of the house. The picnic table is still there, as is the rusted clothesline, hanging loose between the steel posts. A handful of wooden clothespins, blackened with must, are clipped to the lines. He imagines for a second that he's at a crime scene. There was a family in Bentonville who disappeared last year and the nightly news showed the police combing through their house and lawn and the cars parked inside the garage. The family's two collies were discovered dead under the backyard playset, a puddle of antifreeze left in the bottom of their water bowl. He hasn't heard anything more about the family and supposes it's one more case the police have given up on.

"Fuck it." Elijah is messing things up, playing a game. This was his big idea, but now he's nowhere to be found. Layton treads over the weeds, flattened from the Escalade's tires, to the road and looks again at the real estate sign. Why hasn't Gary sold this place? He owned the house, he owned the land, but if he isn't coming back, wouldn't he want the money from it? What's the point of hanging on? Like that missing family, what remains of Gary's life here doesn't make any sense.

Layton gets the shadowy feeling that it was a mistake to have come back here. He could've taken Bobbie just as easily down into the Boston Mountains, on the old 71 that no one but tourists drives, risking their lives on the twisting road to see the fall colors. Elijah wouldn't have known the difference. Or he could've put an end to the cat altogether. She was pickier than a dog—and smarter—but she might've lapped up a bowl of antifreeze, fooled by its sweetness. No one would care, no one would know. The truth is what you want it to be, he's decided, whether it's Sheila wanting to pretend at being normal, at being sanctified, or him pretending to be good, there is no true right or wrong, no action that can't be ignored or forgotten. The lines and the rules are simply things people create to make them feel life is more manageable, less unpredictable than it really is.

He returns to the truck. Bobbie pushes her nose between the wire squares. Cat piss has spilled onto the seats, but there is nothing to do about it. He unclips the latch and opens the door quickly, scooting back several feet to keep clear of Bobbie when she lunges out. But she doesn't lunge out at all, merely sticks her head out and sniffs, pulls her lips into a grimace. Tentative in her movements, she puts one front paw out, then the other, and stands at the edge of the seat.

"Go on." He takes another step back, hoping she'll accept it as an invitation to move. "You used to live here. Get out and go explore."

The cat raises her head and twitches her ears. She seems to have heard something and he holds his breath. It's probably just Elijah tromping around behind the house. He turns to look behind him and the cat leaps into the grass. She hunches down in the weeds, no doubt confused by the feel of so much of it beneath her paws. He shuts the truck door.

He'll have to find Elijah now, who's probably waiting to

jump out and scare him. He's a little shit, Elijah is, just trying to get attention. The night before, Sheila told Layton that Elijah's new interest in Bobbie's freedom had nothing to do with a love of animals. "The kid never even wanted a dog and he doesn't care a thing about that cat. But he's got it in his head that he needs to be around you, Jesus knows why."

"How much more am I supposed to be with him?" Layton said. "He's a teenager and it's summer. He's here all day. He's here at night and all weekend long. What's he want to do? Hang out at the insurance office?"

"That's not it." Sheila waved him off, dismissing him again. Then she tilted her head to the side and gave him a coy smile, as if she were about to tell him something sweet. "He thinks you don't love me."

"How is that his business?"

Sheila's eyes widened and he waited for her to come back with something hateful and mean, something meant to cut him down to size, but that he wouldn't feel at all. She stopped smiling and her chin nearly dropped to her chest as she touched her rhinestoned fingertips to the corners of her eyes. "What?" he asked, but she didn't answer. This morning, she silently put the coffee on and fed the kids before she got dressed herself. Usually, she rattled off her entire to-do list, a litany of tasks that held no interest for him whatsoever. When he'd asked her if he had any clean pants, she'd answered not in her standard tone of annoyance, but in one of resignation.

"Hey, Dad, come back here."

"Back here where?"

"Behind the house."

Layton moves through the grass, the sea of grasshoppers rising and dividing as he goes. He turns the corner to the rear of the house, but no Elijah. The oversized shed that Gary used for drying marijuana stands yards away and, in the far distance, beyond the open acres of pasture and brush, a hill that leads up to a new subdivision. The field is yellow from the late summer drought, but the subdivision's lawns are an almost artificial green. From here, it's a perfect land of neat houses and sidewalks, but he knows that, up close, the shortcuts the construction company surely took—cheap brick veneer, shallow porches, vinyl siding—would leave you feeling like you'd been tricked. Everything about the Estates at Devil's Den is real, solid, with granite countertops in the kitchen and teakwood floors on the front porches—even if what went on inside felt like a life unreal.

He hears the truck door shut and the engine start. He runs to the front, sees the Escalade leaving the drive, Elijah waving at him from behind the wheel. The SUV turns around and starts toward the highway, Elijah hitting the gas pedal so hard that the wheels spin in the dirt, raising a cloud of dust. Layton runs after him, the dust sucking into his mouth and gritting between his teeth, but there's no catching the Escalade.

He left his cell phone in the cupholder, along with his wallet. He has no choice but to walk to some stranger's house to ask for help.

He starts down the road, looking behind to see if Bobbie is following. She isn't. Though she darted away when Elijah took off, she might come back when she realizes she's safe. A house stands at the crest of the next hill. Maybe there will be someone there who can help him, but who knows if Elijah is even heading back home? If Sheila catches him, she'll ask about Layton. She keeps her phone in a little case hooked to her belt, paranoid that someone will need her. Her obsession annoyed him, but now he sees the wisdom in it. Besides his own number, he has only two others memorized: her cell and his parents' landline.

The house is a two-story red brick with tall, white columns along the front porch. The bushes leading up the front walkway are freshly trimmed, a neat row of flat-topped boxwood. To the side of the house lies a horse pasture, and the single horse in it—a palomino, maybe—whinnies at him as he makes his way to the door. When he rings the bell, a chorus of dogs' barks sound inside and he steps back.

The woman who opens the door is flustered with the dogs. "Kennel! Kennel!" she repeats, focused on controlling the dogs tap dancing behind her. When she does turn to him, he sees that she's attractive, a brunette with fair skin, probably only a few years older. He's embarrassed to explain his predicament, but he can't think of a decent story to replace the truth.

He shifts his weight between his feet. "I hoped I could use your phone?"

"Well, sure, I guess you can." She's trying not to show that he's bothering her, he can tell. Really, who needs to borrow a phone these days when everyone has a cell? It *does* sound suspicious. "I'll bring it out to you."

She's more trusting than he would be, but not so trusting as to leave the door wide open while she goes to get her phone. He wonders if she is quickly calling a husband or a neighbor to let them know a man is at her door.

The door reopens and she holds a cordless phone in one hand and, in the other, the leash to one of the dogs, now sitting quietly at her feet. "I've got something on the stove, so you can just leave the phone on the patio when you're done." She points to the wrought-iron table. "I guess you're calling for a ride?"

"I am. I was out here looking at some property and my son ran off in my Escalade."

"Oh." Her eyes widen.

"He's a teenager." He sees himself as the woman does—a potential criminal—and feels his cheeks flush.

"They can about drive you crazy." She gives him a sympathetic smile. "I've got to get back to the stove." The door closes, and the deadbolt clicks.

He sits on the front step and dials Sheila. She never lets the phone go past two rings, but now it rolls to three, four, five. He leaves a message. She could be in the bathroom, although he knows that she keeps her phone with her even when she's on the toilet. He counts to fifty before he dials again. He'll give her another minute and, while he waits, he calls his own number. Elijah may have the decency to pick up, at least to make sure his father isn't hurt. But Elijah isn't answering, either. He calls Sheila one more time, letting it ring enough to roll over to the voice mail again.

It's been years since he called his father for help. They

speak often but their relationship is different from how it was when Layton freely sampled the drugs he and Gary trafficked, when he was dumbly unaware of how dependent he was on others for keeping his life straight. Gary made sure the claims were filed, the distributors paid. At home, Sheila took care of the bills, cooked the meals, kept the kids alive. His father's job was that of a distant shepherd, one quietly reappearing when troubles arose. Layton was responsible only for himself. After he stopped all the drugs, except for the occasional joint, and his head cleared, he was surprised by all that went into the day-to-day management of Insure-U, of what went into being an adult man. He didn't like it, but his father's praise and obvious relief made it tolerable.

He dials the number. Like the woman here at the house, his parents have kept their landline, mistrusting cell phones and regarding them as something to use only as a last resort. On the second ring, his mother answers.

"I need to talk to Dad. Could you put him on?"

"You're not at the emergency room, are you?"

"No, I'm not hurt." His mother had to be sedated the night he was delivered to the ER, beaten and so badly swollen that he was nearly unrecognizable. Wild with grief and worry that he would die, she lost control and went screaming through the hospital. Sheila told him later that by the time they caught his mother and shot her up with Haldol, she'd flipped over a half dozen tables and chairs in the cafeteria.

"All right, I'll get him," she says. In the background, he hears her call out his father's name—Rodney—and his response. Layton can picture them standing by the desk in the kitchen, his mother handing the phone to his father and, as she does, his father leaning down to kiss her on the lips. An affectionate couple, publicly so, they kiss at every departure or return, and also at other small moments throughout the day. He's never questioned it.

"Can I help you, Layton?"

"You can," he says. "I'm stranded. It's a long story, but Elijah's having some problems and he left me high and dry."

"Left you where?"

"Up here by Gravette."

"What are you doing up there?" His voice is stern.

Layton didn't think this through. His father blamed Gary for Layton's beating, too, a belief he revealed only after Gary met with the same fate and then disappeared.

"You're at Gary's old place."

"We're just up here driving around, Dad."

"You know as well as I do there's not one thing to see in Gravette."

"Okay, okay," he says. "But I still need you to come get me. Elijah's run off with the SUV."

"You took Elijah? You know Gary isn't there."

"I know that."

"Do you?" says his father. "You understand this, Layton: Gary is never coming back. He will never be back to that house. He will never be in your life again."

How can he know so much about Gary? The finality of his father's words is disturbing. "I'm not sure about that, Dad," he says. "The house hasn't sold or anything."

There is silence on the phone. His father doesn't know

everything. That house and the little bit of land that went with it is all that Gary had of his life with his own parents— he inherited it when they passed away, his father from a heart attack, his mother from cancer.

"How do you know that, son?"

He feels small, childlike, yet feels a kind of relief, too, a sense that he doesn't own every wrong he's ever done, he doesn't carry them alone. "I guess I don't."

"And that's for the best," says Rodney, a lightness returning to his voice. "Now, I know I come up 49, but you'll have to remind me of the rest."

"I'm sorry you have to do this," he says. "I tried Sheila first, but something must be wrong with her phone. And I don't know what to say about Elijah."

"It's no burden to a father to help his son." Rodney is gentle. "I love you, Layton. You have sons of your own, so you understand what that love is, don't you? How it changes a man?"

His face grows hot and his throat tightens, from shame or gratitude or love. He should've asked the woman in the house for a glass of water. He'll have to wait an hour, probably longer, before his father can make it all the way up from Ft. Smith. After that, they'll have the long drive home, then a confrontation with Elijah and Sheila, his father witness to it all. But maybe that's all right. His father's presence might still the waters, buy him some time to figure out what he's supposed to do.

For now, though, his job is to wait. He sets the phone on the patio table and walks out into the yard. When he nears the edge of the property, the dogs begin to bark inside the house and he guesses the woman has been watching all along, waiting for him to go. He waves at the house. Beside the road, he steps near the ditch, close to the remaining trees to take cover beneath their shade. The air smells of dust and the leaves of hickory trees and the house's freshly cut lawn. He told his father he would be at Gary's, where he could wait without bothering anyone.

He walks down the flattened path at Gary's to the picnic table, sits on top, folding his legs beneath him. He feels a kind of homesickness, listening to the world around him in the afternoon stillness. The cicadas are quieter than they were even a week before, their hum a comfort. His eyes begin to close and he blinks them open. Something moves in the weeds in front of him, the high grass shifting in waves, serpent-like. He holds his breath. It could be one of Gary's exotic snakes, the boa constrictor or python left to grow into a monster here in the woods.

He hears the growl first—not an angry growl, but one of greeting. Bobbie stops in front of the table and sits and licks one of her front paws. She yawns and blinks her eyes. He puts out his hand so she can sniff it, and she does, the wet of her nose brushing his fingers. She comes closer and stretches out below the table's long bench, her belly pulsing with the beat of her heart. He wants Bobbie to stay, but if he moves too quickly, she may change her mind and go.

He slowly unfolds his legs and lies down on the table, flat on his back so that he can see the clouds. He can hear the birds and the insects in the trees, the sound of Bobbie on the ground below him. He's safe here, and he inhales, filling his chest with the warm air. He came here for forgiveness—he understands that now—but he would settle for repentance. He stretches his arms out on either side of his body, palms open to the sky, making himself an offering and a sacrifice to the wild all around.

ACKNOWLEDGEMENTS

Thanks are due to the journals and editors who first published these stories (some in a slightly different form): "Animal Lovers" and "Retreat" originally appeared in the *Colorado Review*, "Deeds" in *Midwestern Gothic*, "This Trailer Is Free" in *Natural Bridge*, "Not From Here" in *Carve Magazine*, and "Pyramid Schemes" in *New South*. "Unnatural Habitats" was published by *storySouth*.

It's been a long and winding road to the publication of this book, but I've been fortunate to make friends who have been there to help me each and every step of the way. Thank you to my writing family in St. Louis: Rebecca Brown Gregory, Sarah Johnson, Myrta Vida, Ron Austin, Leeli Davidson, Kim Lozano, Heather Luby (I do not accept that you have moved to Wisconsin), Emily Grise, Meagan Cass, Jen Tappenden, Aisha Sultan, and Gianna Jacobson. Sara Ross, in particular, deserves my heartfelt thanks for holding my hand and talking me down off the ledge during my moments of panic. I am also grateful to Lee Farrow for a couple of decades of support, and Elijah Burrell for simply being Elijah Burrell. Others have kindly and generously guided me over the years, and I am thankful for the mentorship of Stephanie G'Schwind, Linda Wendling, John Dalton, and last, but not at all least, Steve Yarbrough.

Many thanks to Michael Nye for enthusiastically sharing his insights into the world of publishing and his willingness to commiserate over sports-related injuries. Through the Sewanee Writers' Conference, I've met more good folks than I can name, but I'm especially grateful to Sarah Harris Wallman for her continued friendship, but also for introducing me to Michelle Ross, who read this collection in an earlier form and offered the critical and honest advice that made all the difference. Another Sewanee friend, Louise Marburg, encouraged me to submit to WTAW Press and I thank her for her goodwill, wisdom, and humor. And many thanks to Peg Alford Pursell and the staff at WTAW Press for their faith, patience, and willingness to put this work out into the world.

My deepest gratitude, though, is reserved for my family. My sisters, Carmen and Melissa, know me better than almost anyone and continue to claim me, regardless; I'm lucky to have them in my corner. I am grateful to my parents, John and Carole Mitchell, for keeping me up on the news from home and standing by me through it all. And, of course, I thank my husband, Robert Phillips, who has helped me carve out the time and space I have needed to write and propped me up on those days when I felt defeated. I started writing in the year after my oldest son's birth and, though my timing could not have been worse for learning such a difficult art, I would not have had the nerve to even try before I became a mother. To Duncan and Aidan, my sweet sons, know this: you made me brave.